Deep
IN YOU

THE PHOENIX SERIES BOOK 1

The Phoenix Series:
Deep in You
Deeper in You

POWER. STRENGTH. CONTROL.

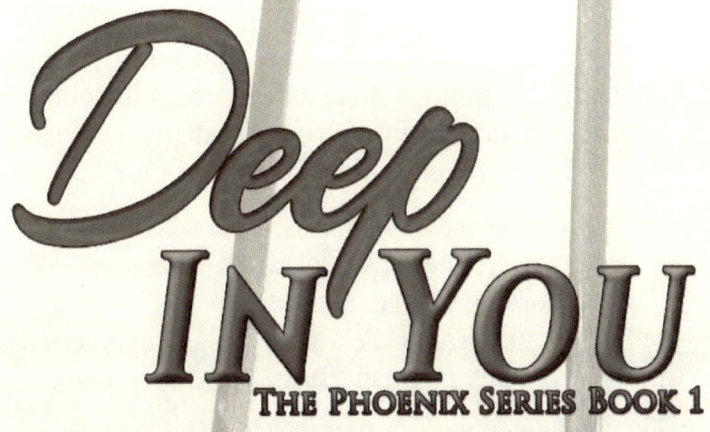

Deep
IN YOU

The Phoenix Series Book 1

DAVID S. SCOTT

Printed in the United States of America

First Printing: June 2016

Published by Seraph Wing Publishing

ISBN-13 978-0-9907111-6-2 (ebook)

ISBN-13 978-0-9907111-8-6 (print)

ACKNOWLEDGEMENTS:

A huge thank you to my incredible wife, Stephanie. Your love and support mean so much to me. Most of this story would not have been possible without your encouragement and faith.

To my personal assistant (PitA), Melissa Ann, how you put up with my nonsense (I was going to use a different word but was told it was bad to curse in acknowledgments) each day is beyond me. Yet here you are, making me write, organizing the street team, and tirelessly promoting and supporting me. You've been with me since the start of this crazy adventure, back when Xander was a tantra instructor. My how things changed. But you stayed with me, encouraging me and guiding me. I can't ever thank you enough.

I'd like to thank my editor, Matt Schiariti, for all your help and ideas. You may have made me wonder if I even know *how* to speak English, but the book wouldn't be anywhere near as good without you so I'm glad to have endured the torture.

A special thanks to the very talented Darkmantle Designs for the wonderful job on the cover and formatting.

To all the members of my street team, David's Decadent Divas, I appreciate everything you do. You ladies promote every day, and have done so even before my books were even close to being released. If it weren't for you, no one would have ever heard of me or my books. Thank you so much for everything.

To my Beta Readers—Melissa Ann, Ella Medler, Elizabeth Booth Bennett, Lacia Carabas, Marcia Mason-Heaston, Tammy Markowski, Terrie Meerschaert, Rachelle Pianalto Jones, Cristiane Karamanolis, Denise Williams, Tosha Merritt Rabideau, Kathy Atwell, Chrisstine Hague Pearce, and Donna Tripi Salzano—thank you for everything you have done. Each and every one of you has touched this book in some way, and helped to make it better.

Last, but not least, a huge thanks to you, the reader. Without readers, there would be no reason for writers to write. I hope you enjoy *Deep in You* and consider leaving a review to let me and other readers know what you thought about this book.

This book is dedicated to Steph and Melissa. Both of you should stop nagging me to sleep. Plenty of time to sleep when I'm dead. Besides, I'll have more time for that now that I'm done writing this book. Theoretically.

Um... right?

TABLE OF CONTENTS

CHAPTER ONE

Power.
Strength.
Control.

These were the attributes I valued, lived by. They had become my mantra.

Power. Watching the gymnasts as a child had fascinated me, and my parents had been quick to capitalize on this and enroll me in classes. It got me out from underfoot, and I loved the feeling of power and strength that coursed through my body. I learned to contort myself into impossible positions and hold them until the exertion almost proved too much... and then push myself even further.

Strength. Gymnastics taught me a lot about myself. I craved a good challenge; the thrill of winning seduced me. I was damned good at it, too. Over the course of my career, I'd won five gold medals and four silver in the last two Olympic Games, as well as countless other awards in other forums. Much more civilized than contact sports, gymnastics tested both my mind and body. On an apparatus, there was only me. Not my competitors.

Not my coach. My greatest opponent was always, and would always be, myself.

Control. Power and strength are great, but without control you run into trouble. I employ control in every aspect of my life. Exercise, my free time, and sex. Especially sex.

My arms and abdominals strained. My spine was held upright, with my legs parallel to the ground as if I were sitting... except I was nearly ten feet in the air, suspending my full weight from two rings hanging from the ceiling in my home gym. I grunted, forcing myself to count. Finally reaching five hundred, I extended my legs farther in front of me and lifted slowly into a handstand. I held that position for a few seconds, then lowered myself down into an Iron Cross formation.

Power. Strength. Control. My body was an extension of my mind. If I could imagine it, I could do it. Nothing would stop me from reaching my goals. Only one thing left of this routine.

I raised back into a handstand and started to spin. Two revolutions, then release. I curled in on myself, tumbled three times, and landed. My right ankle was slightly off, and my leg collapsed beneath me.

"*Shit!* God fucking damn it!"

I dropped onto the ground and folded my right leg to my chest. Fire shot from my ankle into my foot and up toward my knee. Fuck, that hurt.

"You okay, Xander?" My coach jogged toward me, concern etched on his face.

"Do I fucking look okay?" I snarled.

"Let's see it."

I waved him off. Sam meant well, but I really didn't want to be treated like an invalid. He'd been my coach since I was a child. We'd been through everything together.

"Xander, I need to see if you've injured your leg."

I rolled to the left and rose to my feet. My leg still hurt like a son of a bitch, but a glance at the clock told me I needed to get moving. It was Friday night, and I had promised a buddy I'd meet him at a local club downtown for drinks.

"I'll be fine. Don't sweat it. Just a strain."

"Alexander—"

"I said I'm fine. Leave it be."

"Don't start that shit with me, hotshot. You don't pay me to stand to the side and look pretty. This is what I do. Let me see it."

I folded my arms over my chest and glared at him, but remained where I was. Sam squatted next to me and unwrapped my ankle. I always wore ankle wraps on both ankles when working out.

"Flex."

I rotated my foot, wincing. *Sadist*, I thought as Sam pinched and kneaded the top of my foot and ankle.

"Nothing looks or feels broken. I think you're right. It's just a pulled muscle. It'll likely bruise pretty good. You should stay off it."

"I'll get right on that. Tomorrow. I have plans tonight."

"Of course you do."

"I've had worse injuries, you know that. This one is no big deal. Seriously."

"It's a shame that happened. You were looking good up there. Strong. I hate to say this, but–"

"Then don't. I don't want to hear it. Listen, I have to get ready. You can come in and have a drink before you go if you want."

Sam shook his head. "If you're sure you're all right and can manage the stairs, I'll just take off. My wife asked me to pick up some stuff on the way home."

I gave him a brief nod as I limped to my gym bag, passing the pommel horse and beam. He knew the way out.

My two-story house had been custom built per my specifications. The gym took up a third of the space. It housed all of my gymnastic equipment and a selection of weights and bars for strength training. The room had been constructed double-height to accommodate the rings and horizontal bar. The master suite was located upstairs, while a single guest room occupied the ground floor, along with the living area and kitchen. There was a full bathroom on each level, but nothing else. Some of my friends called me eccentric, and maybe I was… but I knew what I wanted and needed. Nothing else mattered. I strode through the large double doors into the house and eyeballed the stairs. I needed to go up there to get my clothes but, for now, decided it would be better to shower in the guest bathroom.

I turned the hot water on as high as it would go, then sat on the edge of the tub to get a better look at my ankle. Yup, Sam was right. I could already see the tell-tale signs of swelling. A few rotations of my foot told me all I needed to know; it was sore, but not broken or sprained. It would end up being an ugly bruise that would ache for a few days. I *should* ice it, but I didn't have time, and heat felt better, anyway. I'd keep it wrapped for a few days, but had nothing to worry about. Once I'd moved it around a bit, I realized it didn't even hurt that much anymore.

I unwrapped my other ankle and stepped into the shower, wincing as the scorching water hit my back. I shifted around so that the spray was concentrated on my leg.

I was no stranger to injuries. Minor ones like this, at least. They came with the territory, but they were annoying. Giving in was like losing, though, and I *hated* to lose… in life as well as gymnastics.

CHAPTER TWO

I pulled up to the club in my electric blue Shelby Mustang GT350R. I loved this car. I drove it the same way I had sex: aggressive yet always in control. The slightly darker blue racing stripes along the hood never failed to turn heads, and the roar of the engine was simply exhilarating. I parked the car at the entrance and stepped out, the oppressive Florida humidity washing over me. I was used to it, though. I'd lived here all my life. I tossed the key to the valet and adjusted my tie. My ankle still ached, but I knew it would until the bruise cleared up. I strode to the front of the line, ignoring the scathing looks from the people waiting.

A glance at the bouncer made him wordlessly lift the velvet rope to allow me access. I gave him a nod as I passed, slipping him a fifty. He'd have done it anyway, but I've found that you get more cooperation when you give them a good reason.

The club pulsed with energy, an almost tangible thing. I knew my friends would be around somewhere, and I would find them eventually… unless I got a better offer. I ambled through the dance floor, moving to the music and grinding with a hot blonde with a huge rack as I passed. She seemed fun but was way too easy. I preferred a challenge.

I approached the bar and settled onto a stool at the far end.

"Xander Phoenix. Been a while since I've seen you here." The bartender was cute and slender with spikey pink hair, tattoos, and lots of piercings. "What can I get ya?"

"Jameson, neat. Make it a double, Chrissy."

She poured the drink while I examined my surroundings. It had been a while since my last random encounter with a woman—at least three days. Practically an eternity. I enjoyed the thrill of the chase, the anonymity of a one-night stand. I never did repeat performances. That was just asking for disaster. No commitments, no mess, no emotions.

The image of long auburn hair and bright green eyes swam in my vision, but I shook myself out of it. *No.* I couldn't think of Faith, the awkward reporter who had once interviewed me in my own home, disarming me with every glance. She was gone. She wasn't even part of the equation and never had been. I'd only fixated on her because I'd never had her. I was sure of it. It did irritate me that no matter how many different women I hooked up with, it was never enough to get her out of my head.

A nearby couple talking together intimately captured my attention. Closer examination, however, proved they may not be as intimate as my first glance led me to believe. The woman was stunning, her dirty blonde hair tied in an elegant twist on the top of her head. She sipped her martini slowly, but never lowered the glass from her scarlet lips. Her deep brown eyes scanned the bar as if looking for an escape. She clearly didn't like this guy and was trying to avoid having to speak to him.

For his part, the guy with her was horrible at taking hints. He leaned far too close, as though he were trying to claim her. He spoke animatedly, and I was able to catch bits and pieces of what he said. Stock market, retirement pensions, insurance premiums. No wonder she wanted to escape; the guy was trying to bore her to death. I signaled to the bartender and got up from my seat.

"Hey, Xander, you made it!" The voice of my buddy, John, filled my ears. I rarely ever saw John outside his shop or his home. He owned a gaming store and practically lived there. I occasionally turned up for a game of after-hours poker, but that crowd wasn't my scene.

"Yeah, I'm here. Listen, it's good to see you, but I can see that a very good friend I've never met needs my assistance."

John followed my gaze. "Already? Damn, you move fast. I think that one's taken, though."

"Not for long. See you around." I gave John the brush-off, prowled my way around the bar, and walked up behind my target.

I deliberately set my drink down and placed my hands on the bar on either side of her, protectively, like she belonged to me. I smiled down at her, resisting taking a blatant glance at the obvious bird's-eye view of her tits.

"Hey, baby, I'm back. Did you miss me? Who's your new friend?"

She blinked up at me, astonished. I winked, took her glass from her hand, and took a long pull. It was sweet and fruity. Definitely some sort of girly vodka martini.

"What are we drinking tonight? This is a far cry from the shots you normally do with me."

This was the moment of truth. She could choose Mr. Retirement Fund… or me. It only took a second before I saw the gears click into place.

"Hey! Glad you made it. Of course I missed you. Why did you keep me waiting? As for this guy? He's…"

We both turned to stare at him.

"I–I'm j-just leaving," he stammered. "It was good meeting you, Lily. I'm sor–bye." Mr. Retirement Fund bolted toward the door.

I stepped up onto the recently-vacated barstool and smiled at her. I finished off my drink and gestured to the bartender, who immediately brought over a fresh whiskey and a replacement martini for my new friend.

"How did you know I don't normally drink martinis?" she asked me once the bartender moved on to another patron.

I smirked. "I didn't. I just wanted him to see I was comfortable taking your drink. Showed him that we were together and got rid of him."

"Who *are* you?" she asked.

"Me? I'm just a guy who likes to help."

"No, really. You look familiar."

"Just one of those faces." I downed the second shot. Here's the thing about me: I don't like to go the easy route. Sure, I used my status and celebrity to skip the line outside, but that's pretty much where I prefer the special treatment to end. I leaned back on my stool and very obviously looked her over from head to toe, enjoying the blush that colored her cheeks. She picked up her martini glass and took a long swallow. Her tongue flicked out to lick her full, perfect lips as she lowered her glass. I found myself entranced. Those lips would be so beautiful wrapped around my cock later.

I cleared my throat. "So, seeing as how I rescued you from a dull evening of stock exchanges and retirement plans, do I get to know your name?"

She chuckled, a full, throaty laugh. "You were listening that closely, were you?"

Shit. I'd lost focus. I never should have let that slip. I was rapidly losing the upper hand. I leaned forward, my blue-gray eyes boring into her brown ones. "No. I know his type."

"What type is that?"

"The boring nine-to-five type. They think the way to get to a woman is through their bank account. They may be stable, but rarely have the kind of money needed to *really* impress anyone. Simple, uninteresting, predictable. I'm sure he seemed like a nice guy, but he probably doesn't know how to please a woman in bed."

There it was. Her eyes darkened, and she licked her lips again. "And I suppose you do, then?"

"What do you think?"

"I think you're overly cocky if you think I'm nothing but a cheap blonde bimbo who will just fall into bed with you at the snap of your fingers. While I appreciate your help, I see no reason why you'd be considered an improvement."

Oh, I liked this one. She had spirit. I leaned toward her, conspiratorially. "It's not cockiness if it's true."

"So you *do* think I'm a cheap blonde bimbo?"

"Not at all. I can tell that isn't the case just looking at you." I checked her out again. "Beautiful. Classy. The kind of girl who knows the difference between a mustang and a mule."

She snorted. "Definitely cocky… and corny. I know your type."

"I would be happy to back up my claims."

"You should be so lucky."

She sounded tough, but she had put her glass down and was giving me her full attention. "I think *you're* the one who brought up the idea of us going to bed together. *I* merely spoke of your friend's apparent inability to please a woman."

"He's not my friend."

"I'm very glad to hear that," I murmured, knowing she'd be the only one who could hear me. She didn't answer, but she didn't have to. I knew I had won. Game. Set. Match. "Dance with me."

She looked a little surprised. "What?"

I grinned. "Dance with me."

I stood, and pain shot through my right ankle. Not too bad. Tolerable. Dancing probably wasn't the best idea I'd ever had, but my ankle was wrapped up, and I was determined to close the deal. I held out my hand to help her from her seat. She hesitated, but I stood still, determined. I waited for her to make the right decision.

She relented and slid down from her barstool, refusing my hand. I gestured for her to lead the way, but she stumbled. Without thinking about it, I was at her side, assisting her, my hand at the small of her back.

"Wow. Those martinis hit you out of nowhere," she said with a giggle. "I've got this. Just felt weird for a moment."

"Maybe I like helping you," I answered, flexing my fingers against her spine. Together, we made our way to the dance floor.

If there is one thing I've learned over the years, it's that, given the right partner, most women love to dance. They love being able to rub their bodies all over a man, drive him to distraction, while remaining in a safe and very public environment.

I led her onto the dance floor just as the song transformed into a heady, sexually charged tempo. Not slow enough to be awkward, but not so fast as to deter intimacy. *Perfect.*

She looked a little self-conscious, facing me with uncertainty, like she didn't know where to start. People jostled us from every direction. A woman with bright blue hair came up to my left and gyrated against me, but I ignored her. I pulled my mystery friend—Lily, I'd heard that asshole call her–by the wrist into me, spinning her around to face away from me and holding her to my chest. I lowered my face to her ear. "Stop thinking so much. Just let the music take you. Lose yourself in its rhythm."

She shuddered in my arms. I started to dance, rolling my hips into her. She responded, finally stepping free and surrendering herself to the music. Now that she had relaxed, I could see that she was no novice to dancing, just as I'd expected. She kept her back to me, which gave me the chance to appreciate her perfect ass. Fuck, this girl could move. She knew exactly what to do to make my blood simmer.

The music changed to a slower beat. I closed the distance between us and gripped her waist, pulling her into me. She stiffened as she felt my cock hard against her ass, but quickly relaxed into my embrace as we swayed slowly to the music. I leaned down to her ear once more.

"Do I get to know your name now?" I murmured, my voice husky.

She turned around and gazed up at me. She placed her hands on my chest and slowly, seductively moved them up and around my neck, allowing me to pull her close and wrap my arms around her waist. "Lily Campbell."

I smiled down at her. "Xander Phoenix."

Her eyebrows lifted. "*The* Xander Phoenix? The X-Wing? The man who flies?"

"One and the same. But that's business; this is about pleasure. Don't think about any of that."

"I knew you looked familiar. I've seen–"

I cut her off with a kiss. I knew what she'd seen, what they'd all seen. I didn't want to talk about gymnastics now. Don't get me wrong, I love it. I like being able to control my body to do these things, enjoy the admiration I get. It just wasn't my focus here in the club. My interest was only in the beautiful woman in front of me.

I deepened our embrace, capturing her mouth with mine, claiming her. She was delicious; sweet with a slight taste of martini. My tongue caressed hers, danced with hers. My pulse increased to dangerous levels as she moaned and matched me stroke for stroke. I retreated slightly before driving into her again, our mouths a mimicry of what I wanted to do to her with my body. Everything else fell away–the club, the people pressing into us from all sides, the noise, all of it. It was just me and her, doing positively indecent things, uncaring of who saw us. Unable to resist, I roughly groped her breast through her shirt.

She pulled back, her eyes dark, hooded. We both breathed heavily, and my head spun. I felt drunk off her pheromones. She took my hand and led me off the dance floor through the club's exit.

The humidity washed over us as soon as we stepped free of the air-conditioned building, breaking the spell. I signaled to the valet, noticing she didn't make a move. "Your car?"

"I took a cab."

Interesting. She'd expected to leave with someone… or she'd expected to get so drunk she couldn't drive. One of those. I supposed I shouldn't judge. I'd intended to leave with someone, too. My car was brought up. I held the passenger door open for her before getting in the driver's seat.

She watched me, desire apparent on her face. She didn't offer any directions, so I steered the car onto the freeway, shifted into sixth, and headed toward my place.

CHAPTER THREE

I pulled into my circular driveway, parking and killing the engine. "This is it."

Lily stared through the windshield. "It's not as big as I expected."

"That'll be the only time you say that to me tonight." Her face flushed crimson, and I chuckled. "I don't need a lot of living space. I'm the only one who lives here. Come on." I got out and walked around to open her door for her.

"What a gentleman," she said as I helped her out of the car and led her to the house.

"At times. Would you like a tour?" At her nod, I continued, gesturing with my chin. "Straight ahead is the living area. There to the right is the kitchen, and here to the left is the guest room. The master suite is upstairs. Simple. Would you like a drink?"

"Yes, please."

I selected a sweet red from the refrigerator and grabbed a couple of glasses.

"What's through those doors?" she called from the living room.

I joined her and handed her one of the glasses. "My gym."

"Can I see it?"

"Maybe later."

"Please?"

"Later. I have far more important things on my mind right now. To us." We clinked our glasses together and drank. "So what brought you to the club tonight without a car, Lily Campbell?"

"I… I don't know. I just decided to shake things up. I just broke up with my boyfriend and decided that I didn't like who I saw when I looked in the mirror. I wanted to be someone else tonight, so I called a taxi and the rest you know."

I'll never understand why women bring shit like that up to men they've just met. Whatever. I'd be her rebound fling. After tomorrow, I'd never see her again, anyway. "Do you like who you've decided to be tonight?"

Her eyes lost focus, not really looking at me. I noticed that they were red and strangely dilated.

"Do *you*?" she asked.

"Hey…" I cupped her chin in my hand to force her to look at me. "Very much. Out of all the women in the club, *you* stood out to me." I set down my wine and rose to my feet, holding my hand out to her. "And do you have any idea what you were doing to me when you moved your body against mine? Tour's not over yet. You haven't seen the upstairs."

I placed her glass on the table and took her hand, tugging her hard into me and kissing her. Her hand snaked around my neck while both of mine dropped down onto her ass. I kneaded her round curves, my tongue plunging insistently into her mouth. My body came alive. Tingles raced all over my skin. My cock throbbed for her. She knew it, too. She grinned against my mouth and hummed appreciatively. Her other hand reached between us and found my erection, stroking me through my clothes.

Shit. We weren't going to make it upstairs; I needed her now. Right now. I felt reckless and lightheaded, and it made me behave in a way that wasn't normal for me. I had somehow allowed her to take control, and I couldn't have that. My house, my life, my rules.

Making a snap decision, I changed direction and almost carried her toward the guest room. Without breaking our kiss, I unbuttoned my shirt and removed my tie. Shrugging them off, I wrenched myself away long enough to tug her shirt over her head, then pulled her back against me. My tongue pressed into her mouth, stroking, exploring.

Then she did something I never expected. She closed her lips around my tongue and sucked hard. A strangled groan ripped from my throat.

I unhooked her bra and practically threw her onto the bed, enjoying the way her breasts bounced as she fell backward. I yanked a condom out of my pocket, tossed it on the bed, and followed her down to reclaim her inviting lips. My hands found their way to her tits. She arched her back to press herself into me as I pinched and rolled her nipples between my fingers.

I allowed myself a few moments more to enjoy her breasts, then kissed my way down her belly. I unfastened her jeans and shoved them roughly to the floor, along with her panties and strappy shoes. My clothes soon joined them.

Her hands found my chest and lightly skimmed my pecs. Goosebumps rose up all over my skin. I couldn't wait any longer; this girl would drive me mad. I reached down and felt her slick entrance. She was so ready. I couldn't wait to be inside her.

"Your tight little cunt is soaking for me, Lily. So needy... you can't get me inside you fast enough, can you?" Her nails dug into my skin. I grabbed the condom and ripped it open, rolling it on with well-practiced movement.

"I need you, Xander. Now, please."

I lined myself up and thrust into her. We both gasped. I had been right; she was incredibly tight, her pussy squeezing me. I paused, buried balls-deep inside her. "Did I hurt you?"

She scratched at my back like a tiger while she pressed her heels into my ass, encouraging me to move. "I'm fine. Please…"

I began to move, slow and deliberate at first, quickly gaining speed as we lost ourselves in each other. Lily screamed, her nails raking my back. I moved my forearms to press into her shoulders, allowing me to thrust even harder, plunge myself even faster. I pivoted my hips to be sure my cock hit her g-spot.

"Oh… God, yes. Fuck! Just like that," she moaned. "Like that. Don't ever stop."

There it was. "Don't stop." Those words had me fighting for my self-control. No way was I stopping until she was finished, no matter how crazy she made me, how much I needed to come. I put my mouth to her ear. "You feel so tight. So incredible. I can't get enough," I growled. "I could fuck you again and again, all night long. That sweet cunt is heaven for my cock."

"I'm so close."

"Let go, baby. Come for me." I bit down on her lower lip, sucking it into my mouth as I felt the first tremor wrack her body. Her pussy squeezed me in rhythmic bursts.

"Yessss," she moaned.

I pumped into her twice more, then pushed as deep as I could and stilled. My whole body tingled in the split second before my orgasm ripped through me. We rode out our climaxes together, my feathered kisses soft on her lips.

"Xander?"

"Mmm."

"That was…"

I withdrew myself from her depths and rolled to the side. I gathered her in my arms, and kissed her just under her ear. "I know, Lily. I know."

Chapter Four

The black water churns and foams. Debris litters the nearby beach below. I'm standing on a pier with a broken railing, staring down in horror. She's gone... gone. I couldn't save her. Not this time. She wouldn't listen. She never listened. My poor sister...

I moaned and rubbed my face, disoriented.

Where the hell am I?

My head felt fuzzy. I blinked up at the ceiling, confused. It looked familiar. Right... the guest bedroom. I was in my guest bedroom having yet another nightmare about my sister's death. I rolled over and found myself staring at the back of someone's head. Damn, I couldn't remember her name. What was it?

Oh, right. Lily. Lily Campbell.

Why was she still here?

The memories slammed into me. How much did I drink? I added it up, but still had no idea how I ended up so out of it. Two double shots of whiskey and a few sips of wine should not have had this effect. And what the hell was that last night? I'd felt so out of control, like I was outside my own body. That never happened to me. At least I'd had sense enough to put on a damned condom.

I sat up, shaking my head to clear it. Something was definitely wrong.

"Lily?" The sound that came from my parched throat didn't sound like mine. It was hoarse, dry, a stranger's voice. She didn't move. I turned her onto her back. "Lily?"

Fear washed over me. I sat up and loomed above her naked body. She was so pale, and I couldn't see that she was breathing. There was a dried puddle of vomit next to her, with a small chunk of something I'd rather not dwell on.

"Lily… Lily, wake up. Please wake up." Fighting my panic, I placed my fingers on her jugular vein. Her pulse felt rapid and weak, but it was there.

I was torn. I barely knew this woman, and I was pretty sure we'd been drugged. It would explain both the way I felt and the state she was in. Should I call 911? Should I call the police? I'd make headlines nationwide. *Damn it!* How could this even have happened? Not the club, surely; that was an upscale club, not a dive. Certainly not the kind of place where you expected this sort of thing to happen… but to think otherwise meant it had been in my personal, sealed bottle of wine. It had to be the club, only why would anyone drug us both?

It had to have been the martini. I drank some of it, but not as much as she had. Had to be. I needed answers, but I wouldn't get them until she was awake. I carried her into the bathroom, stepped over the tub, and braced myself. I turned the shower on.

Freezing water washed over us. I gritted my teeth and stood steadfast. Lily moaned and squirmed in my arms. I nearly dropped her, but managed to hold on tight.

"Hey, wake up, sleepyhead. We need to talk."

"Fuck you, Xander. What have you done to me?"

I was so relieved she was talking that I couldn't be insulted at her accusation. Whatever it was she'd been given couldn't have been *too* terrible; she remembered who I was, where she was, and she could talk. "Let me guess. Your head hurts, you feel sick, and you feel like you were hit by a truck, right?"

"So you admit it. Put me the hell down," she snarled. "What, didn't think your macho act was enough to get in my pants? You had to drug me, you twisted asshole?"

"Relax, Lily. I didn't do this, honest. I would never do this to anyone. I couldn't…"

I trailed off. My sister was dead and buried, and it was ultimately drugs that killed her. I had always been anti-substance abuse, but after I lost her it had become almost a religion for me. I couldn't explain any of that to the woman in my arms, though.

Lily went silent, but not because she was digesting what I'd said. She'd passed out again, still under the spray of the water.

"Damn it, Lily. Wake up!" I forced her into a standing position and held her there.

She groaned. "Xander... what is going on?"

"Come on. I've had enough of the water. Will you at least *try* to stay awake? Let's talk about this." I shut off the water and helped her out of the tub. "You need to keep moving. Stay awake. We were drugged, Lily. The only drinks we shared were my personal sealed wine and your martini at the bar. Let's assume for the sake of argument that it's the martini."

"Okay," she mumbled.

"Focus, Lily. I know the bartender, and I doubt she tried to drug you. Tell me about the guy you were with. Mr. Retirement Fund.

"I... I don't know. I can't..."

"Lily, did you turn your back on him at any point?"

"No."

"Did you get up for any reason?"

"No. Of course not."

"Not even to go to the bathroom?"

"I'm not a complete idiot. I know not to… to…"

Her pale complexion lightened further. I tightened my grip around her in case she was about to pass out. If she passed out again, I would call for an ambulance, to hell with what the press would think.

Her mouth moved but no sound came out. Her bloodshot eyes darted up to meet mine. That's when I realized she wasn't fainting. There was guilt written all over her face.

"Tell me."

"I'm such an idiot. I… I–"

My lips tightened, drew into a thin line. I wanted to yell at her, to curse at her. But it wouldn't help. Damn it! I had a qualifier coming up, and that meant I'd be tested. Who knew what that asshole had drugged her with? My career could be destroyed.

I didn't know what to do. I wondered if I should just go ahead and take her to the hospital so we could find out what we were dealing with. I shook myself; that was a terrible idea. I should call Sam. At least he knew how to be discreet.

That thought flooded me with guilt. This wasn't about me. If she wanted to find this guy and press charges, I needed to help her.

The fact that we woke up at all was a good sign, but now what? Call the cops, fill out reports, interviews, deal with the press… a shiver ran down my spine. Xander Phoenix, victim of a date rape drug. I'd never live it down. Also, there was the fact that some of them are used as enhancements for competitions. Illegally, but still usable. Some would never believe I had nothing to do with it. I'd be the next Lance Armstrong.

I stared at Lily, still leaning into me. "Do you want me to take you to the hospital?"

"I don't know. Do you think I should?"

No. "Yes. You probably want to press charges, and that means getting a full medical workup."

"What will happen then?"

"The hospital will call the police. We'll have to give statements. They'll start an investigation."

"I don't want that."

"You don't want this guy to be caught? Off the streets?"

She shook her head. "I don't want them to know how stupid I was. He seemed okay. I thought I could trust him."

"You aren't the first he's done this to, I'm sure."

"I can't. I don't want my life pulled apart for everyone's amusement. I'd be a laughingstock. Especially since… never mind. That's not important. What *is* important is that I feel better already. There has to be a better way."

I couldn't do it anymore. I couldn't try to talk her into doing the right thing when I really just wanted this whole problem to go away myself. I nodded. "Okay."

I'd get Sam over here and find out what was going on. I helped her into a chair, then fished out my cell from the wad of clothes on the floor at the foot of the bed. After tapping out a quick text, I tossed it onto the bedside table.

"If we aren't going to the hospital, looks like you'll be staying with me for a little while."

"No need. We can call a cab."

"Do you have a roommate?"

She started to shake her head, but froze, a look of pain and fear on her face. "No. Well, yes. I do, but she's not... um... she's not there right now."

"Then you should stay. I need to make sure you're okay. Hell, I could use the company. You can keep an eye on me, too."

"You seem fine."

"I probably am. If I am right and it was the martini, I only had a sip. Still, my head isn't quite right, so better safe than sorry."

She lowered her gaze. "Okay."

"We could try drinking water to flush our systems, but honestly, it probably just has to run its course." I wanted to believe that the water would help, but I really wasn't sure. It at least sounded good.

She didn't say anything, so I took that as agreement and helped her up. "Let's go to the kitchen. I'll get you some water and see if I can find some clean clothes that might fit you."

"What's wrong with my clothes?" she asked, still dazed. "I don't think I can drink anything."

"If you can't, you can't. This room smells like vomit. Let's go out there."

I assisted her into the living room and helped her get settled on the couch. I gathered the empty bottle of wine and glasses from the coffee table and threw them in the trash, just in case.

From the fridge I grabbed a couple of bottles of Smart Water, the only kind I ever bought. Maybe the electrolytes it advertised would help flush the shit from our systems. Reluctant at first, Lily took a sip. She didn't bring it back up right away. I took that as a good sign.

"I'll be right back. I'm just going to get some clean clothes. I'll see what I can find for you, too, if you'd like." I climbed the stairs, ignoring the protests from my ankle. I grabbed a pair of sweat pants out of my dresser and tugged them on, commando. For Lily, I found a small T-shirt and a pair of shorts I hadn't worn since high school. I washed my face and brushed my teeth. As an afterthought, I added the toothbrush and toothpaste to the pile of stuff.

Lily hadn't moved. She stared glassy-eyed at the doors to my private gym, chin resting on knees pressed to her chest. I passed her the items I'd brought down for her.

"Closest I could come up with that might fit."

"Thank you," she said sullenly, without looking at me.

"You'll want to put those on."

"Okay." She still didn't move.

"Sam will be here any minute."

That did it. She stiffened in surprise, but straightened up to look at me. "Who?"

"My coach. Get dressed."

She jerked the shirt over her head. "You *called* him?"

"Of course."

"So much for needing *me* to keep an eye on you."

I sighed and grabbed the nearest water bottle. "Look. We can trust him. More importantly for me, though, is that he'll test us. If word gets out that I took drugs, intentionally or not, I could be ruined. I need to know what we're dealing with."

On the plus side, my head was clearing by the moment. I actually felt almost normal.

"Xander, I changed my mind. Maybe we should go to the hospital."

"Why? I thought we agreed that was a bad idea."

"I want to get tested."

"I *told* you Sam will test us. We'll have the results back just as fast and a lot more discreetly."

She cocked her head. "Why don't you want me to see a doctor? I don't know this Sam. How can I trust him to be honest? How can I know he isn't covering something up?"

I crossed my arms, quiet fury building up inside. The tension around us was palpable. Had anyone else walked in right then, they would have been able to *feel* the force of my rage. "Explain what you're implying, exactly. What would Sam not be honest about?"

"How did I not see it earlier? You said, 'let's assume for the sake of argument that it's the martini,' and I accepted that. But why *should* I accept it? It makes just as much sense for it to have been the wine. *Plus,* you've been encouraging me to not go to the hospital this entire time. You want your friend to clean up your mess. Admit it!"

"I'm not going to admit it, because there is nothing to admit. That bottle was sealed. This is asinine." My hands clenched into fists. How *dare* she?

"I don't know you any more than I knew that guy. Unlike you–a self-absorbed jock who just wanted to get into my pants–he was at least a gentleman."

"So the theory you've decided to run with involves me bringing you into my home, then drugging you to get into your pants... even though you'd already *chosen* to come here. I hadn't realized that your goal when we left the club was to come over to play *Monopoly*!" I spat the last word, my temper spiking. I wanted to get away from her. Now that she'd officially accused me, Sam would have my balls if I kept talking to her about this. I would need to get my lawyer over here, but for now I just wanted space.

"*My* plans were irrelevant, since I was drugged." She jabbed her finger in my chest. "You took advantage of me!"

I reared back like she'd slapped me. "What the actual fuck, Lily? I told you before, I had nothing to do with this. I had no idea you were drugged, so how would I have known I was taking advantage?"

I raked both my hands through my hair, trying to calm my rage. My attempts proved useless, however. I had to get away from her.

I stormed into my gym and slammed the doors behind me. I knew I should have been keeping an eye on her, but she certainly argued like she was lucid enough. I no longer gave a shit whether Sam tested her or not. If she stayed, I'd get her tested. If not, she was on her own.

She had some balls accusing me of taking advantage of her. She'd agreed to come here on her own; I hadn't forced her. If she hadn't been fully in control, how could I be blamed? I'd drunk from the same glass.

I approached the pommel horse and lovingly stroked the leather, taking in the smell, letting the familiar setting comfort me and calm my frazzled nerves. I'd always felt at peace in the wide open space beneath the high ceilings of my home gym. It had anything I could ever need.

Who was I kidding? She was wrong to accuse me of taking advantage, but it didn't mean I hadn't done so. That didn't sit well with me. I had banged a woman who had been literally unable to say no. There was no way I could justify this away. Bottom line: the fact that there had been no intent to force myself upon her would *not* stand up in court.

I was so screwed.

I needed to work off some steam, so I sat down to stretch.

The opening of the door signaled Lily's arrival. "The fuck do *you* want?" I snapped. "You aren't welcome in here."

"You said last night that you'd show me your gym."

"Yeah, well, that was before you accused me of raping you. Get the fuck out."

Lily stared at her bare feet, which traced patterns in my padded floor. "I'm sorry I said those things."

"What?"

"I'm sorry I said all of that. I know it had to have been the martini at the bar. I'm freaked out and I felt bad for lashing out, so I came—"

"You're more than welcome to leave whenever you'd like," I interrupted. "You didn't have to stay out there."

"—to find you. But isn't your coach coming to test us?"

"He's coming over. He'll also test you if that's what you want. Tell me something, Lily. Would you have *rather* been taken home by the asshole that drugged you?"

The doorbell rang before she could answer. "I'll be right back. Don't touch *anything*," I called over my shoulder as I walked away.

The doorbell rang a second time. "Keep your damn shirt on, Sam."

I opened the door to find him carrying a black sports bag, a disgruntled look on his face.

"The fuck you doing texting me this early on a Saturday? Do you realize that my hair was completely black when we met? Every single one of these gray hairs is your fault. What the hell do you need drug testing gear for? What did you do? You know better."

I chuckled. "Get in here, asshole."

"I see nothing funny about whatever your situation is right now."

I shut the door behind him. "Okay, here's the story. I met a girl—"

"I don't like this story already."

"Shut up. I met a girl at the club last night, saved her from some boring ass. Only it turns out the boring ass wasn't quite so… well, he drugged her. And me, as collateral damage. I need to know what it is."

Sam eyed me, his pale eyes sharp. "I've seen you look worse. But let's see what the tests say before I go making any mystery diagnoses. How'd he get you, too?"

"Drank from her glass."

"You drank from her—what the hell, man? You *know* how irresponsible that was. You *never* drink out of strange glasses when you're at a God damned night club! Hell, it's best to not drink anything there unless it's from a sealed bottle."

"You are aware we don't live in Mexico, right? That stuff about 'don't drink the water unless it's bottled' doesn't apply in Orlando."

"It does for *you!* When are you going to learn that as an athlete, you need to always be two steps ahead of the game? Don't take risks. Don't gamble with your career. All you need is a competitor or someone that doesn't like you to slip you something before a qualifier. I am just blown away by how stupid that was!"

"Calm down, Sam. Mind your blood pressure. I actually feel much better than I did; almost normal. Lily isn't, but she *is* improving."

"Fine. You know the drill." He handed me a cup. "Cap it nice and tight. Don't want that shit leaking on me."

"First, come meet her. Keep an eye on her for me while I'm in the can." I dropped my voice. "She's acting crazy. I'm hoping it's the drugs and wears off soon." I wanted to tell him what she had accused me of, but I knew he would flip out. It may still be necessary to involve him, but I hoped her apology meant she was becoming more rational. If so, I'd get her tested and send her home. I'd speak to my lawyer on Monday about whether he thought I needed to get her to sign anything.

"Crazy, how?"

So much for that. "Nothing, man. Just talking nonsense. Let's get this over with. The sooner I get her out of here, the better."

Sam and I walked into the gym. Lily had sunk to the floor next to the pommel horse but was awake and alert.

I dropped to my knees in front of her, taking in her vacant stare. "I need you to get up, okay? You need to take the drug test. This is Sam, my coach. He has connections at the lab, so this will all be very discreet. He's going to explain what you need to do, okay?" I looked up. "Sam, this is Lily."

I left the room while Sam talked to her, their voices diminishing and disappearing as I reached the bathroom. Water covered the tub, floors, countertops, walls, everything. We had made a huge mess. Not the way I would have pictured us showering together. I quickly filled the cup and capped it, leaving the sticker that was supposed to contain the depositor's name and personal information blank. Sam would deal with that however he chose.

This whole thing sucked. This was not how I'd envisioned spending my Saturday. All I'd wanted when I met Lily was a quick hookup, some hot sex, and then we'd part amicably and never see each other again. Instead, I ended up dragged into some deep shit involving felonies and God only knew what else.

I grabbed a towel and dragged it across the floor, mopping up most of the mess. The room needed to be completely cleaned, but I'd deal with it another time. I tossed the towel in the hamper and went to go find the other two.

Sam was right. What I did *was* stupid, and I could only hope that I didn't end up paying for my idiocy with my career.

I really hated when Sam was right. If I admitted it, he'd never let me live it down.

CHAPTER FIVE

"I'll call you as soon as I know anything. The lab's closed today, but my buddy says he'll open up and run a couple of stat tests. I told him it was important. Do you two have any plans?"

"Well, actually, Sam," I said. "I—"

"That was a rhetorical question, Xander. You two are to stay here until I get the toxicology reports back. Got it?" He raised his eyebrows. "Once we know what we're dealing with, we'll decide what steps to take next."

I nodded. "Thanks, Sam."

"You'd better. I'm pulling a lot of strings to get this taken care of today. Pleasure meeting you, Lily." Sam inclined his head to her, then headed out.

"I should be going, too," said Lily.

"I don't think it's a good idea. You heard the man. You should stay until we hear back." My words didn't match my convictions. I wanted her to go. To hell with what Sam thought. The sight of her was an annoyance I wanted removed. I didn't sign on for any of this. I had just wanted to fuck her and be done with it. I needed her to leave, but knew she had to stay. I couldn't have her getting into trouble or talking to people before I knew what we were dealing with.

I again considered contacting my lawyer, but I trusted Sam. He'd contact him if he felt it was necessary. Dragging in lawyers only made you look like you had something to hide.

"What happened to your ankle?" The question came out of nowhere, surprising me.

"What?"

"Your ankle is wrapped. I noticed this morning."

"I wrap both when I work out."

"That's not an answer."

I quirked my eyebrow at her. "Bad landing before I left for the club last night. Just a strained muscle, nothing serious."

She nodded. I was surprised that she had noticed. Neither of us had been very observant yesterday, and today there were plenty of distractions.

"What's going to happen next, Xander?"

"Well, Sam will call us back and tell us what it was. Then we'll research what to do about it. Don't worry."

"If I stay, will you show me one of your routines? I could use the distraction."

What? No. I'm not a trained monkey performing tricks.

"We'll see," I answered.

Perhaps it would be a fun diversion to give her a private show.

Wait. What the hell was I thinking? I was not an adolescent, needing to show off to some girl in hopes she'd go out with me. I was Xander fucking Phoenix. I needed to get my shit together. *If* I gave her what she wanted, it would be because it was a diversion, like she'd said. Nothing more.

We sat down together on the couch. I turned to face her and brought my right leg up between us. Slowly I unwrapped the bandage around my ankle.

The skin underneath displayed a nasty green bruise. Gingerly I rotated my foot. It wasn't too bad; I'd done worse to myself. The appearance was the worst of it. A glance at Lily found her staring at me with a look of horror on her face.

"Hey…" My words forced Lily to look me in the eyes. I smiled reassuringly at her. "What's wrong?"

"That looks horrible, Xander."

"Just a bruise. It doesn't even hurt that much. I've had worse."

She swallowed hard and nodded a little, then tucked her feet beneath her. I rewrapped my ankle and watched her for a bit.

"So you have me at a bit of a loss, Lily Campbell. I know your name. I know you have stunning brown eyes and, based on the condition of my back, are quite a tiger in bed. I know you like fruity martinis and you don't like being bored by losers in clubs. I think that's about it. You know quite a bit more about me."

"You also know that I recently broke up with my ex."

I sighed. "Yes, I suppose I do remember you saying that."

"Why'd you react that way? Would you rather we were still together?"

To be honest, I didn't give a shit *who* she was with. I knew that wasn't the answer she wanted to hear, though.

"No," I said. "I think my feelings on that are quite clear. I was just hoping you'd tell me a little more about yourself. What makes you tick?"

She stared at me, fear written all over her face. I was becoming more confused by the moment.

"I'm a journalist," she whispered, turning away from me. She twisted her hands nervously in her lap, and her complexion turned ashen.

My brow furrowed. Had she written something bad about me in the past? Why did she look so freaked out? "Are you okay? Are you going to be sick?"

She squeezed her eyes shut and shook her head. I placed my hand over hers. I couldn't help myself. "You ashamed of being a journalist?"

"Not normally, no."

"But now…?"

"I'm a journalist for *CaS*."

There it was. The reason for her shame and hesitation all made sense now. *Celebrities and Sinners*. A tabloid.

Shit! She worked for a tabloid, and here we were together, drugged. The many ways this disaster could be spun out of proportion rushed through my brain all at once. One thing was certain: Sam needed to hurry with those reports.

I realized I was staring at her, so I cleared my throat and attempted to act normal. "So, a journalist, huh?"

"It's still considered journalism."

"Really? Writing goss–I mean, good writing for a public magazine or newspaper should always be considered journalism. Of course."

"That's true." She looked up at me then. Her face was still pale but she seemed to be sizing me up. Grabbing her water bottle, I held it out to her and stood. "Well, come on, then."

"Where are we going?"

I gestured toward the gym doors. If we'd needed a distraction before, it couldn't compare to how badly we needed one now. "A deal's a deal."

We re-entered my gym, and I considered all the possibilities. I opened a cabinet drawer near the doors and removed my ring grips. I pulled them onto my hands and glanced at her. "Ladies' choice. What do you want to see?"

She looked around, her eyes lighting up. "What would you like to show me?"

"Up to you. Rings, of course, are what I'm known for but, as I'm sure you know, I always try to qualify for the all-around. I enjoy floor routines and the horizontal bar almost as much."

"Rings, please, Xander."

I nodded, pleased with her choice. "Anything that you see here is off the record."

"You think I would write about this?"

I chuckled. "Nope. I don't think your readers would care about my workout routine. I think my competitors might, though, so better safe than sorry." I covered my hands in chalk and approached the apparatus. I gazed up at it with affection. Sometimes it seemed I was born for rings, my favorite event. I mentally ran through my routine, focusing my attention inward and getting in the zone. Time always seemed to slow way down whenever I prepared for a performance; all the chaos of my life would fall away and leave me with a feeling of peace.

I braced. Mounting the rings apparatus was always easier with Sam around. I'd have to jump and catch them just right without his guiding hands.

I lifted one arm up. Unnecessary in this forum, but a good habit to keep. I bent at the knees and sprang into the air, catching both rings. Instinctively my hands shifted to adjust my grip a few times, then, when I was ready, I straightened my arms to hang free. I pulled my feet in front of me and rose into a handstand. I counted to ten, then dropped down until my body was parallel to the floor, facing down. Adjusting my grip once more, I lifted myself as if I were doing a push-up into a higher position. I lowered again to hang all the way down before rolling over to perform a slow somersault. That done, I straightened out and held for a few seconds. Taking a deep breath, I spun around three times in quick succession, reversing my hands effortlessly each time, finally ending in the Iron Cross formation.

My muscles twitched as I heard a gasp. Sweat beaded on my brow, yet I held the pose. I needed my focus back. Why was she able to distract me? I'd blocked out cameras, cheers, and arenas filled to capacity in the past, but one woman managed to sneak into my brain in the middle of a workout. Must have been the drug remnants in my system.

Wait, wasn't I supposed to be counting this position? Great. My distraction was worse than I thought. At least Lily didn't know my routine. I'd just do the shorter competition version, rather than my workout version. I began to prepare myself for the landing, assessing my foot. I lifted myself back into a handstand, then started to spin. Once, twice, and I released, curling in on myself and tumbling three times before my feet hit the mat.

Pain shot through my right foot, but I'd stuck it. I froze, my knees bent. Yup, that shit hurt, but it was manageable. I straightened up and flung my arms into the air. Perfect.

I smiled at Lily as she applauded. She looked a little happier than she had before we came in here. More color to her cheeks. Maybe the adrenaline helped.

All at once, I was able to see her in the same light as I had in the club. Despite everything we had been through, all the things we had said, the attraction was still there. Everything faded, her accusations, my fury, all of it. I plucked the ring grips off my hands and dropped them on the floor, then closed the distance between us.

"Xander, that was—"

I interrupted her with a rough kiss, forcing my tongue into her mouth. My hands cupped her ass and pulled her tight against me. This was more like it. Now she was where *I* wanted her, and not arguing with me. I was instantly hard as stone, and I wanted her to feel what she did to me. I wanted her. *Now.*

"You took advantage of me…" The memory struck me, and with it, my anger returned. With a snarl of frustration, I tore myself away from her and struggled to catch my breath. I was far more winded from kissing her for less than a minute than I was from that entire rings routine.

"Why did you stop?"

"This was wrong."

"Wrong?"

"Yes. You're still sick. I've already been accused of taking advantage of you once. I won't allow it to happen again."

I also shouldn't lose focus of the fact that we were only in this predicament because *she* couldn't be bothered to follow simple safety protocols when drinking with strangers. This whole situation was all *her* fault, for all she'd blamed me for it.

"I'm sorry I said that. I didn't mean it, I swear. Besides, I'm feeling much better."

"That's nice." I wandered over to the parallel bars and pulled myself up to work through my

49

routine. My body switched into autopilot as my mind wandered off.

I never should have given in and kissed her. She seemed the needy type and, make no mistake, I did not want her thinking she would have a chance with me. I had no intention of fucking her again, no matter what my traitorous body wanted. I didn't do repeat performances. I was just waiting for Sam to call so I could send her on her way.

I released my right hand, flipping backward through the air while spinning around blindly to catch the other bar, then lifted into a handstand.

"You know, you never see this side of you on the television."

Her voice startled me, wrenching me from my thoughts. I jerked, losing my position and crashing down to the padded mat. Knowing what was coming, I relaxed my body to soften the impact.

"Oh my God, are you okay?" She covered her mouth, obviously trying not to laugh. She had some nerve, laughing at me.

"I'm fine. I know how to fall. I just prefer not doing it. Which, by the way, wouldn't have happened if you had kept quiet. You startled me."

"I startled you? How on earth could I have startled you?"

"Must be the drugs. My head isn't in the game." That was my story and I was sticking to it. I'd performed in front of millions. There was *no* excuse for one woman to have gotten to me like that.

"I see." Lily paused. "I was just kidding around anyway. I'm sorry. I didn't mean any harm, it's just..."

"Just?"

She blushed again. "On television, you're always wearing your uniform. Here, nothing but your loose workout pants, and they leave little to the imagination."

I glanced down at my still-obvious erection. Bastard wasn't going down at all, and her proximity wasn't helping matters. I swallowed hard. "Sorry."

She licked her lips, her eyes dark. My breathing quickened in response, though I tried my best to appear unaffected. "No need to apologize. It turns me on," she said.

She reached out a hand to help me up, but I grabbed her and dragged her down next to me. "So let's talk about that, now that you've gotten me down here."

"I got you down here?"

"That's right."

"Looks like you got down here all by yourself."

She leaned forward and kissed me. I made a half-hearted attempt to back away, but she followed me, and who was I kidding, anyway? A gentleman would have better restraint, but I'd never claimed to be a gentleman... at least, not when it came to conquests. I hummed low in my chest, my tongue claiming hers while her hand trailed down my chest. I *never* did repeat performances... but perhaps, given the circumstances, I could make one exception.

Last night didn't count, anyway. Neither of us were at our best, and she *did* seem like she felt better.

My breath caught as she slipped her hand into the waistband of my sweats and tentatively stroked my length. Her fingers felt tantalizingly cool, but not too cold. Lifting myself up a little, I pushed my sweats down just enough to give her easier access, then drew her back into our kiss, demanding her attention. My tongue set a tempo as I thrust it in and out of her mouth, while the hand on my throbbing shaft slowly changed to match my pace. I moaned as I felt her confidence building, and lowered my hand to massage her breast.

"Squeeze it, Lily, just a little harder," I murmured. "Mmm... just like that."

"Xander, I'm so wet for you, I want to taste you so bad."

Her words nearly drove me insane as I plunged my tongue back into her mouth. Her hand tightened around me slightly more as she jerked me off faster and faster. She settled into a rhythm, switching it up every few minutes, bringing me closer and closer to the brink. Each change felt more intense than the last, and I knew my release would be soon. It was too much, too good, the contrast of her soft lips and tongue versus the tightness of her fingers.

"Lily," I gasped, panting, "you'll make me come. I'm almost there."

She grinned against my mouth, encouraged. "Good. Those sounds you're making are killing me. You're so hard, and I keep picturing how you would feel inside me. It's all I can do to not finger myself right now."

I moaned and reached for her, but she shifted away, a mischievous look on her face. All I was able to reach were her breasts, which I again took full advantage of.

"Oh fuck. Higher. Squeeze the tip. Don't slow down."

She immediately complied, almost letting go as she hit the sensitive head with almost all of her fingers.

"Oh fuck! Oh fuck, yes!"

"My mouth is watering. I want to taste you so bad."

I released her breasts and gripped her hair, yanking her head down toward my waiting cock. Her warm, wet mouth enveloped me, welcomed my hard shaft. I didn't waste any time and thrust my hips upward, fucking her mouth. Her tongue swirled up and down, in contrast with her hand around the base of my dick.

"Suck it, baby. Suck it hard."

Her cheeks hollowed as she did as I instructed. My eyes rolled back into my head as she leaned forward and swallowed me. The head of my cock shoved deep into her throat, all the way back to where the hardness of the top of her mouth gave way to the softness of her throat.

I gasped as my orgasm struck in pulsating waves. She continued to suck me, swallowing as my come spurted powerfully down her throat. I cried out, the sensations becoming almost too much to bear.

I squirmed from her grasp, then leaned forward and kissed her, basking in the warm afterglow. I felt relaxed, lethargic... but I wouldn't give in. Not now, not with Lily here next to me, wet and practically squirming for my touch. I had a reputation to uphold. I moved lower and nuzzled her neck, scratching her with my stubble and biting down softly on her flesh. She gasped and arched her back, her hips jutting forward. That was all the invitation I needed. I dragged her shirt over her head and bent down to draw one of her erect nipples into my mouth. I bit down hard and swirled my tongue around it.

Lily gasped and jerked back. I glanced up at her, capturing and commanding her gaze. "Did I hurt you?"

"Yes, no. It hurt, but it… but don't stop."

I paused for a moment, regarding her, then tugged her shorts down and off. I settled myself between her legs and ran my finger over her slick folds. She was drenched, absolutely soaking, just as she'd said. I gave her a wicked grin as I traced the edges of her pussy lips with my first two fingers. I toyed with the thin strip of trimmed hair and brushed my thumb over her clit. Her breath caught.

"Mmm… someone wants me, doesn't she?"

"Yes," she whispered, looking embarrassed by my question.

"What was that? I couldn't hear you." Without awaiting her answer, I plunged my index and middle fingers deep inside, entranced at how slippery she felt.

"Yes!" she hissed. Her back arched upward, granting me better access. I pumped my fingers into her hard and fast as I dropped down and sucked on her swollen clit, my tongue flicking her teasingly. "Oh God, fuck. Xander, it's so good. It's—"

I pulled my fingers out and sat up, breathing hard. I skimmed my hands over her thighs and smiled.

"What? Why did you stop? It was so good; I was getting so close," she whined.

"Shh. Relax. I've got you." Sticking my fingers in my mouth, I moaned in appreciation. "Do you know how damn good you taste? Here. See for yourself." I trailed my fingers between the cleft of her breasts and up her chin. She moved in for a taste, but I pulled my fingers away, enjoying the tease, the anticipation.

I grazed my thumb over her clit, barely touching it. She groaned and tried to press into me, but I backed off, having none of it. When her breathing steadied, I lowered myself down and lapped at her juices. I flicked my tongue around her pussy lips, then plunged it inside, trying to consume every bit of her essence. My thumb found its way back to her clit and massaged her firmly.

"Oh my God. Xander…" Her lips parted in a silent scream, her hands clenched into fists at her sides. Her legs on either side of me began to quiver, so I roughly pulled away again. "What the hell? Why did you stop?"

"Because I can."

"Fuck you, Xander."

I smirked. "Oh, yes, baby. I love when you talk dirty to me."

She glared. She was so damned hot in her fury, and I was captivated. I wanted to see how long I could keep this up, but I sensed she would get pissed off before much longer. I was used to calling the shots, though, and I loved driving her crazy.

Her gaze dropped to my cock. I was hard again; seeing her so needy, so desperate for me made me want her in ways I was probably better off with her not knowing. Loving the hungry way she watched my every move, I gripped my hard shaft firmly in my hand.

"You want this?"

"Why? You just going to deprive me again?"

"Oh, I'll let you come. I'll let you come when I think you've earned it."

I stroked myself a couple more times, then settled myself between her legs once more. I licked her from her entrance all the way up to her clit, which I paused to pay special attention to. Her entire body twitched each time I licked her as though she had been shocked. Slowly I inserted my fingers inside her and curled them to find her g-spot.

"Do you know how hot you are right now? So wet, and this beautiful clit is swollen with desire. It's intoxicating."

"Xander, you'd better not be toying with me again... *ahh*... I'm warning you... oh, fuck, harder."

"All good things," I toyed with her clit, and she moaned, "to those," more pressure on her most intimate spot made her grind her ass into the mat, "who wait." Her thighs locked around my head, determined not to let me escape. Luckily for her, I was through fucking around. I gripped her hips and pushed my tongue inside her, licking and sucking. I relished the taste of her, enjoying the way she bucked beneath me as she hurtled toward ecstasy. Her thighs quivered, and I knew she was close.

She squirmed, pumping her hips and grinding my face. "Ohh, shit. I'm going to come. Don't you fucking stop, Xander. Don't you dare fucking...oh, fuck!"

A garbled moan escaped her throat, her pussy tightened rhythmically. I continued to lick her, extending her orgasm.

"Ahh, Xander, I–"

I tore myself away, forcing myself free of her legs. "Scream for me, Lily," I said as I climbed up her body and pressed her lips in a brutal kiss, letting her taste herself. She was still coming down from her climax, her beautiful eyes unfocused. Unwilling to wait a moment more, I lined myself up and plunged deep inside her.

"Oh, God!" Lily shouted as my cock caressed her sensitive nerves.

I silenced her with a kiss. "Shit, Lily. Your cunt is so warm and slick. Perfect. I'll never get enough." I forced my tongue into her mouth and began to move inside her. She cried out every time I thrust inside her.

Why had I never brought a girl in here sooner? Sex on the springy floor of my workout room was raw, sexy, and… and… I lost my train of thought as Lily lifted her legs, pulling them over my shoulders. Fuck, this girl was hot.

I stopped and pulled out. "Turn over," I gasped. "Get on your knees."

Lily hurried to do as I commanded. I gripped my dick and gently rubbed the tip against the entrance to her tight little ass, noting how she tensed up as I did. I moved down and shoved myself back into her slick pussy, slapping her ass as I did so. She cried out, a wail of ecstasy.

"Oh shit, that was hot. You liked that, too, didn't you?" I spanked her again, enjoying the satisfying smacking sound.

"Yes," she murmured.

I gripped her hips and thrust her back to meet me. "What was that? I couldn't hear you. Did you like me spanking you, Lily?"

"Yes!" she yelled, only it sounded more like a garbled moan, staccato from the force of my pounding thrusts.

"That's better." Reaching one of my hands around in front of Lily, I found her clit and pressed hard each time I pumped inside her. My other hand continued to hold her exactly where I wanted her. It was so good. Too good. Shit.

"Lily, you're gonna come for me now."

"Yes. God, yes. I'm close."

I rubbed her clit in a circular motion. I felt a warm tingling starting; I knew I had seconds. "Fuck. Me, too. I can't stop. Come *now!*"

I pulled her hips back as I thrust forward, falling over the precipice of my orgasm. The blood rushed through my ears. Lily tightened around me, squeezing me, milking my dick. My eyes forced themselves closed. When I felt her relax beneath me, I withdrew and dropped onto the mat next to her, pulling her against my chest.

CHAPTER SIX

My phone rang. I felt around at my side before realizing the sound came from a good distance away. I rose to my feet, careful not to wake Lily, and jogged over to the infernal sound. The name on the screen told me it was my coach.

"Talk to me." I stepped through the double doors into the living room.

"Just got the results back from the lab. You tested negative. Well, trace amounts of Gamma-hydroxybutyrate, but so slight that it wouldn't flag a positive. She, on the other hand, came out very positive for the same substance. Not dangerous levels, but definitely ingested. Here's the good news: GHB doesn't stay in the system very long, twelve hours at the most, usually, so she's probably already negative. It could have been a lot worse."

Relief flooded through me. I was clean. Lily was going to be okay. Maybe this wouldn't turn into the publicity nightmare I'd been afraid it would be. "Gamma-hydroxy…"

"GHB is a lot easier to say. Lot of dirtbags using it these days because it's hard to prove. By the time the victim realizes they've been drugged and gets an order for a test, it's already gone."

"I *know* what it is. One of the drugs I can get busted for. It's considered blood doping."

"Yes. Like I said, though, you tested negative."

"It's a hallucinogenic and increases libido and energy. Christ, man. If I hadn't intervened…"

"If you hadn't intervened, she'd likely have been taken advantage of by some *other* person she didn't know while she was too vulnerable to resist."

I flinched. "That was low, Sam. Even for you. You think that hasn't been hanging over my head?"

"Hey, Phoenix, you didn't know. Whoever spiked her drink did. Not your fault."

That may be, but the fact remained he wasn't wrong. I had fucked her last night when she wasn't in any condition to say no. She may have never come here, had she not been drugged. Small consolation that this meant she had been clean the second time.

Sam continued. "The question now is, does she want to call the cops and pursue this? I can bring the lab reports. I can't *guarantee* you wouldn't get dragged into it, but your clean toxicology report will at least keep you from being ruined professionally."

"Let me ask her what she wants. She's a reporter, so she's in the public eye like me. I doubt she'll be interested in word getting out that she was given a date-rape drug in a bar. Hang on to those reports.

Don't let anyone else see them. I'll let you know what she says. Oh, and Sam?"

"Yeah?"

"Thanks."

"Don't mention it, hotshot. Just do me a favor and, for the love of God, be more careful in the future. You go to bars and drink from a stranger's glass, and anyone can spike your drink."

"Fuck, Sam. You know I can't live like that. If I question every single person's motive, they've won."

"Just be more careful." Sam disconnected.

I tossed the phone on the couch and turned to see Lily pulling the shirt I'd loaned her back over her head. She'd already put the shorts back on. I smiled at her, and she walked straight to me. I sure hadn't expected any of this when I left with her last night. I figured we'd have some fun and she'd leave like all the rest. Well, she was still going to leave, just a little later than planned.

I wrapped my arms around her and sniffed her hair. She smelled like lavender and sex, an intoxicating combination. "That was Sam."

"I figured. What did he say?"

"You tested positive for a substance called GHB. Among other things, it's a date-rape drug. I think our friend Mr. Retirement Fund had a Plan B for the evening in case you shot him down."

She shuddered, so I tightened my arms around her. "Am I going to be okay?"

"You're fine. No lasting harm. Don't worry." I paused, still dwelling on the conversation I'd just had with Sam. "Besides, you came home with me and didn't get dragged off to who-knows-where with him."

She smiled, but it didn't reach her eyes.

"Look," I continued, "it's already a little past three o'clock. The drug is undoubtedly out of your system. You're going to be fine, I promise. You don't even need any medical attention. GHB doesn't stick around long. Sam wants to know if you want to call the cops. Maybe they can find that guy."

She shook her head. "No, please. I don't want anyone to know that I was dumb enough to leave my drink with a stranger. I'm just glad it wasn't something worse."

"It's your call. I guess we know why he spooked so fast and ran off. Here I thought I was just that intimidating." I winked, trying to break the tension. I should probably have encouraged her to call the police, but to be honest, I didn't want the attention. That guy was still out there, though. Still preying on women in bars. He could have *ruined* my career. If I ever saw him again, he'd regret that.

I sat down on the couch, pulling Lily with me. "How are you feeling, anyway?"

"Dazed, I think. The last twenty-four hours have been... interesting. My boyfriend–um, ex-boyfriend–dumped me, I went to a bar intending to get drunk, was instead drugged by a creep, and taken home by a celebrity."

"Your boyfriend dumped you *yesterday?*"

She nodded against my chest and sniffled loudly. *Great. Now look what I've gone and done.*

"He said... he said..." She shook her head and buried her face in my side. I stroked her hair while she cried. "I'm so sorry. I didn't mean to fall apart."

"Hey, it's okay. I get it." I really didn't. This was why I avoided messy relationships. It was amazing how quickly I'd become uncomfortable. The conversation had started to feel forced. Now that I knew she'd be okay, everything felt... over. Must be time for her to go home.

"I guess I should be going, Xander. Thank you for everything." As if on cue, she pushed away from me and stood. "Let me just go find my phone and I'll call a cab."

I rose to my feet. "I'll drive you."

"You don't have to. It's okay, really. I don't mind calling a taxi."

"And I don't mind driving you. I needed to go out today, anyway. I have some errands to run. It's no trouble."

She relaxed and smiled. "Okay, then. If you're sure. I'll just go get my clothes on and we can go."

"Sounds good." I ascended the stairs to get dressed, my emotions in disarray. Why did I want to drive her home? I *should* have been happy she was leaving and call the taxi *for* her. It was... guilt. I felt guilty because I'd banged her when she couldn't say no. And, if I were honest with myself, the fact that I didn't know whether she would have come here had she not been drugged was a blow to my ego.

I had fully intended to take her straight home, but when we got in the car, I heard her stomach grumble loudly. I realized I had been a poor host. On top of everything else, Lily had been drugged, could have been raped and turned over to some human trafficking organization or killed, and then I had tried to starve her. Come to think of it, I was starving, too. I pulled into the nearby IHOP. Not glamorous, I know, but convenient.

Despite the gaping chasm of awkwardness between us, I found myself strangely drawn to her. She challenged me even while at her worst, and she exuded sex appeal. I wished I could read her mind, wished I knew if she regretted coming home with me. Not knowing, in itself, felt almost like a rejection, made the sex we'd had in my gym feel like it was only born out of convenience.

I cleared my throat. "What are you thinking about?"

She shook her head slightly, snapping out of it. "Oh, I'm sorry. This was a mistake."

"What was? The restaurant?" I snorted. "I admit it wasn't the best choice, but it was right here—"

"No, not that. All of this." She waved her hand back and forth between us. She regretted meeting me in the first place. I was filled with self-loathing, an unusual feeling for me.

"I see…"

Lily paled, seeming to realize what she was saying. "No, I just meant…" She sighed. "Listen, I was at work yesterday when Michael—my ex—came to see me. He asked me to go talk to him in private, but I was working and told him I was busy. When he didn't leave or say anything, I asked him if something was wrong. I looked up into his eyes and didn't recognize him. He called me a frigid, manipulative bitch and said that we were through.

He told me he was hooking up with Allison… that he'd… he'd…"

Tears streamed down her face, and she buried her face in her hands. I stared at her, at a loss for what to do.

"He'd been with her, behind my back, for weeks. How could I have been so stupid? How could I have not seen? She'd been cold to me lately, but I figured something had been eating at her. I just had no idea it could have been my boyfriend of a year that was the one doing it."

I walked around to her side of the booth and sat next to her, wrapping my arms around her. She buried her face in my chest and shook with silent sobs. I didn't know what to say, so I said nothing, just sat there and rubbed her back and arms. Inside, I seethed. The emotions shocked me. Guilt for what happened in the last eighteen hours was one thing, but I wanted to find this Michael and punch him for hurting her. She'd been through enough, damn it. I allowed myself the fantasy while I held her. He'd be standing there, and *bam!* Right in the nose. He'd collapse in a heap on the ground while I stared down with contempt and–

"I'm sorry," she murmured. "I'm sure you don't care about all this stuff."

"I do, actually. What happened next?"

"Well, the whole office was staring at me. Allison walked in and saw us there together and sidled up next to him with a horrible look on her face. I just grabbed my purse and ran out. I may not have a job anymore." She pulled a tissue from her purse and blew her nose. "Even if I'm not fired, how can I show my face back there?"

"Allison works there, too?"

"Yes. I went home with the intent of eating lots of ice cream and crying the night away. Tears I had plenty of, ice cream not so much. So I decided to dress up and party. Being myself was painful, being someone else for a night seemed like a better idea."

My jaw tightened. Nobody deserved a day like that, and I knew I hadn't helped. I pulled her to my chest and breathed in her fragrance. "What are you going to do?"

"I don't know. I guess I have two choices: I can go back there and face them all, or I can start looking for a new job. I don't know how I can face them. Nothing like being the center of office gossip at a gossip column, but if I don't, I have no idea how I would make ends meet." She sighed. "One minute I was working on the article that would land me the promotion of my dreams, and the next minute everything fell apart."

My mind spun, trying to find a way to fix this for her, a virtual stranger to me. The only ideas I could come up with were nothing short of insanity, so I dismissed them and didn't say a word. Luckily, my thoughts were interrupted by the waitress bringing our food before I could say anything we'd both regret.

With a pang of remorse, I left her side to sit across from her. She offered me a weak smile. "What about you? When was your last relationship?"

"I've never had a serious relationship."

"What?" She dropped her fork onto her plate with a clatter.

"That surprises you?"

"Frankly, yes. I always see women with you on television during your meets."

"Well, I suppose 'never' is kind of a misnomer. I had a girlfriend in middle school and the beginning of high school. That said, I've *never* been interested in tangling emotions with sex."

Her face darkened. "I see."

I frowned. "You just broke up with your boyfriend yesterday. When you left the bar with me, were you looking for a serious relationship?"

"I was drugged when I left with you," she snarled. Her tone made me wince.

"Back to that, again? Fine. Were you looking for one when you left for the bar?"

Her shoulders slumped. "No." Her voice was small.

"Didn't think so. You went to that bar looking for a rebound. You found one." I chewed my food thoughtfully. "I've never been into attachments, and I've always liked it that way. That said..."

"Yes?" she prompted.

"I wouldn't mind seeing you again sometime." The truthfulness of that statement surprised even me. Something had shifted in me since our encounter in my gym. I wasn't going over all romance and commitment, but I hated that she would look back on last night as the night I took advantage of her. I wanted her to *want* to see me again, even though I'd never wanted that with anyone else. On top of that, the idea that she would go back to work on Monday, miserable, stuck in a continuation of the hell she'd found herself in, hurt me. I'd added to this. Like she'd said, she was drugged when she came home with me. I owed it to her to help fix this.

"Why?" she asked.

"I'm not sure," I answered slowly. Well, it was honest. "I think we were good together, Lily. What did you think?"

Her face lit up. *Wow.* She was naturally beautiful, but something about the way her eyes sparkled when she smiled like that blew me away.

"Well?" I prompted.

"Sex was never that good with Michael. It was always about him and his needs. If I finished, too, so much the better, but if not, it didn't matter. With you, it was… very different." She whispered the last few words, staring at her food as if it were the most fascinating thing she'd ever seen.

"Different?"

"Very."

"A good different, I hope." *Please say yes. Please tell me you don't resent me for what happened.*

She took a swallow of her drink. "That's for me to know and you to find out."

We finished our food in silence. When the bill was paid I stood and held out my hand to help her up. "I'm not going to lie. There's something about you, Lily Campbell. I've never felt the slightest inclination to ever have a second chance with anyone… until today."

I opened my car door for her, but instead of getting in, she moved to the side and leaned against the car. She looked me up and down, sizing me up.

Her lips curved. "I'll think about it." She climbed into the car, leaving me staring after her.

What? What did she mean she'd think about it? She'd been pretty clear that she'd wanted more, that she wanted to see me again. That she'd hated I wasn't the relationship type. I blinked, suddenly realizing my mouth was left hanging open. I shut it, then gently closed her door.

We drove in silence as I pondered what her game was. I suspected she had done that because she assumed I was a man who liked a challenge. Damn. If so, she'd played me. Worse... she was right. It was working. Her vague answer only served to make me want to demand she see me again.

She directed me to her apartment building, and I found a parking spot. After a minute, I got up and walked around to open her door. I was at a bit of a loss. What should I do now? Should I follow her to her door? Should I say goodbye here? This was all new to me. I watched her, trying to follow her lead. She fidgeted with her purse, looking for her keys. She smiled up at me. "Thank you for saving me."

"Lily, it was my pleasure." I cleared my throat.

"Maybe I'll see you later."

"Umm... can I get your number?" Fuck. That was awkward. Suddenly I was a teenager again, instead of an experienced, grown man of twenty-seven. I could practically feel the acne and gawkiness popping out. Reaching into her purse, she pulled out a business card and placed it in my hand. Then she leaned forward and closed her eyes.

I didn't need to be asked twice. I closed the remaining distance and crushed her lips to mine. I stroked her lower lip with my tongue, demanding entrance, which she granted. I reached around and gripped her tight ass, pulling her hard against me. Her hands came up and cupped my face. My cock awoke and pressed with delicious firmness between our bodies. I wanted more. She moaned into my mouth, causing my heart to race. I ran my hand under her thigh, urging her to lift her leg up and around my waist. She leaned back against the car, and I loomed over her, boxing her in. I pressed my hips into her, humping her, rubbing my throbbing erection so near to where it wanted to be. She groaned, sending my pulse into overdrive.

After what seemed both an eternity and a brief second, she pulled away. We were both gasping for breath. "Wow," she breathed.

"Yeah." She had flecks of green in her chocolate-brown irises. I was sure I hadn't noticed those earlier, and I was spellbound. I released her leg, and she reached down to cup the front of my tented pants. I sucked my breath through my teeth. In that moment, I'd have done anything she asked of me.

"Better stop that," I rasped, capturing her hand in mine. "My control is hanging on by a thread. I'm about to bend you over the hood of my car and fuck you right here where the whole world can see."

"Oh, fuck…"

"Yes, so unless you're prepared to invite me in, I suggest you run along like a good girl."

Panic briefly flickered across her face. The emotion was gone so fast it left me doubting whether I'd seen it. She reached up and gave me a chaste kiss on the cheek.

"Goodbye," she whispered. Then she broke away and walked quickly into the apartment.

I shook my head as she vanished from sight. This girl was going to be my ruin; I just knew it.

CHAPTER SEVEN

I climbed back in the car and adjusted myself. I would have been far more comfortable had I left my workout pants on instead of wearing jeans. I looked at the business card she'd given me. Was it possible she just wanted me to try to reach her at her office, even though she may or may not return there? I relaxed when I saw her cell phone number had been printed on it as well. Shifting the car into reverse, I left.

I hadn't really had any errands to run. Honestly, I wanted to spend more time with her. What was happening to me? I wasn't even sure who I was anymore. I should have been working out today; I had a huge qualifier competition coming up in a little over a month. Reaching the freeway and shifting into sixth, I pointed the car toward home.

At home, I changed and went to the workout room, trying to focus on my routines. But even without Lily's presence, I was distracted. I could still feel her hand on my cock, could still remember the way she looked and sounded as she got off. *Fuck!* I let go of the rings and dropped lightly to the floor, careful to land most of my weight on my uninjured foot.

What was I going to do? Her memory consumed me. I walked over to my weight collection and selected a pair of dumbbells. Sam would kick my ass if I did serious weights without him there as spotter, but this would work.

I had to get her out of my system. I'd found myself asking to see her again, and I was pretty sure I couldn't blame the GHB anymore. *That* wasn't me. I had her number, but I needed to forget about her. Getting tangled up with a woman like her was not smart. How the hell was I going to fix this?

Banging her hadn't done the trick; I'd have happily gone another round or two. Maybe I needed to find someone else to get her out of my head. I nodded. That was a good idea. I'd go back to the club tonight and pick up another chick. I paused. What if I ran into Mr. Retirement Fund? Well, I'd cross that bridge if I came to it. He needed to be taught a lesson, but I was the wrong man for that job, unfortunately.

A glance at the clock told me it was nearly seven o'clock. I put the dumbbells down and went upstairs to take a shower. I stripped off my clothes as I waited for the water to heat. I regretted not showering with Lily. Standing together under the frigid spray had been a poor substitute. I stepped into the hot water and relaxed in the steam. I pictured her, soaking wet with water dripping down her skin. I'd trap her against the wall with my arms, and she'd stare up at me with those doe eyes of hers.

There I was, thinking that way again. I really needed to stop. Gripping my erect shaft, I stroked myself. I started slow but soon began pumping faster and harder, the water from the shower a poor replacement for Lily's natural juices. I'd pin her arms above her head and feast on her neck. She'd groan and lift her legs when I'd urge her to wrap them around me. I pictured the sounds she'd make as I buried myself deep inside, imagined her nails at my back, her teeth on my shoulder, the sound of her screaming my name.

My breath hissed out through my teeth as I found my climax, my jizz spurting down the drain. I continued to stroke myself until the last tremor faded away, then leaned forward against the wall to catch my breath. Shame consumed me. I hadn't felt guilt after jerking off since I was a teenager… but there I was, embarrassed and ashamed because I was imagining someone I had just decided to forget about.

"I need to get a grip," I whispered to myself. "I'm fucking pathetic." I finished showering and got dressed for another night at the club.

CHAPTER EIGHT

Like the night before, the club was hopping when I arrived. I tipped the bouncer and strolled inside without a second glance. Unlike my entrance yesterday, which was more laid back, today I strode in with purpose. I could feel the eyes on me as I approached the dance floor, and I smiled, happy to be the center of attention. That would make things easier. I approached a tall redhead and placed my hands on her waist, grinding with her to the beat of the music. She could move and was probably hot in bed, but too much about her was fake. Everything from her brown roots to her permanently shocked expression that betrayed her use of Botox to her ball-shaped boobs. You'd think she would have at least hired a decent plastic surgeon. I moved on from the Versace-wannabe and headed straight for the bar. The spiky-haired bartender from the night before was still here, so I signaled to her.

"Mr. Phoenix, this is a surprise. Two nights in a row, no less."

"Hey, Chrissy. My usual, please." She poured the whisky and started to move away, but my hand on her wrist stopped her. She arched her eyebrow and her blue eyes darted to mine.

"Take your hand off me." Her voice was calm, dangerous.

I quickly acquiesced. "Sorry, but I needed to ask you a question, and didn't want to be overheard."

She frowned. "What kind of a question?"

"Do you remember the girl I was drinking with yesterday?"

"Raspberry martini chick?"

"That's her." I shouldn't be doing this. Shouldn't be talking about Lily, shouldn't be associating myself with her, shouldn't be thinking about her. I *really* shouldn't do what I was about to do. "There was a guy sniffing around her before me. Nervous, balding, bad comb-over."

"I saw him. I've seen him around a few times. Not regularly. Why do you ask?"

"No major reason. I need to talk to him, that's all. When do you normally see him?"

She frowned. "I can't think of a pattern that I could identify. Some are predictable. Like you, for example. When you *do* come around, it's always a Friday or Saturday evening, but never both. Except right now. I guess there's a first for everything. That one turns up on week nights. Sometimes three nights in a row. Sometimes only once. The day differs. Sometimes he doesn't come back for weeks. Anyway, if I see him, I'll let him know you're looking for him."

I waved my hand, dismissively. "Don't bother. Probably better if I *don't* see him. I'll take care of it if I do."

"*What?* I don't want any trouble in my bar."

I downed my drink in one long pull, and slammed the glass down.

"There won't be. Don't worry, Chrissy. Thanks for the talk." I turned around to survey the dance floor once more, only to do a quick double-take.

Lily was here, dressed in a miniskirt and tight tank top. In the span of a second, the whole club seemed to fall away. The music muted, the people disappeared, and the only ones here were her and me. Her dark blonde hair floated loose about her face, her makeup was smoky and dark. That was it. The last straw. My entire purpose of coming here was blown to shit. I wanted *her*.

What the hell was she doing here? She had been drugged in *this* club last night. Why would she risk it? There were other clubs. I watched her closely, stepping back toward the bar and trying to make myself invisible behind other people. She searched the crowd, looking nervous. She *should* be nervous. Coming here again was stupid. I'd figured this would be the one place on earth she *wouldn't* be.

I realized there was another girl with her. This one looked foreign. Her tanned skin, dark eyes and black hair made me think she might be of some sort of Middle Eastern descent. What were they doing here? Could Lily be after the same thing I was? When I had dropped her off this afternoon, it never occurred to me that I might see her again today. Her friend grabbed her by the wrist and hauled her onto the dance floor. She started dancing right away, but Lily just awkwardly swayed, looking around in every direction as though she expected a monster to jump out at her at any moment.

Ah, hell. I pushed off the barstool and stepped back onto the dance floor. Some guy was all over Lily's friend, but my eyes were only for her.

I snuck up behind her and placed my hand on her slender waist. Rolling my hips into her, I murmured in her ear, "Stop thinking so much. Just let the music take you. Lose yourself in its rhythm."

Lily gasped and spun around, her hand raised as though she would slap me. Her eyes were wild.

"Surprise." I lifted my hand to her chin and gently closed her mouth before covering her lips with mine in a lingering kiss.

She pushed me away. "What are you doing here, Xander?" she hissed.

I gave her my most charming smile and pulled her back into my embrace, dancing with her. Now that she was in my arms again, she seemed to remember how to move.

"Looking for you," I lied.

"Right. And you just happened to come *here* looking for me."

I frowned. "Well, frankly, that does confuse me. Why *did* you come here?"

"Well, since you came looking for me, why don't you explain that?"

I rolled my eyes but said nothing, waiting.

Finally, Lily relented and gestured to her friend. "Amara wanted to come. I may have told her I'd met you here, and so she wondered who else might come here."

"Did she?"

"Yep."

I watched her as we continued to dance, ultimately forgetting what I was doing and stopping. I drew her close and pulled her tightly to my chest, one hand at the small of her back and the other tangled in her hair. Our lips met as though an invisible force drew us together. No one else in the club mattered. Lily was my drug, and I didn't know how to cure my addiction. I wasn't sure how I could become so obsessed in just one day, but the hard facts were that I was. Maybe I could still blame the remnants of the GHB?

She moaned against my lips, and my already hard cock pulsed against her belly. I wanted her badly. Why were we here in this club?

"Oh my God! You're him!" The unwelcome interruption distracted me. I looked up to see Lily's friend staring at me. With regret, I released Lily, admiring her lips that were swollen from my kiss.

"Alexander Phoenix. Pleased to meet you." I held out my hand.

"Amara Dagher, reporter for *Celebrities and Sinners*. I know exactly who you are, Xander." She flashed her teeth at me. "Do you mind if I call you Xander?"

She reached for my hand but stumbled forward as she was jostled by a dancer. I caught and helped steady her.

"Oh, I'm so sorry," she said, but made no move to separate and stand on her own.

I smiled thinly. "Think nothing of it. We should get off this dance floor before someone gets hurt." I released Amara and turned to Lily, pretending not to notice the death glare she shot her friend. I placed my hand on the small of Lily's back and escorted her back to the bar without waiting for Amara.

I saw three chairs together and headed for them, holding out the chair in the middle for Lily. *My mother would be so proud,* I thought. *See? I do know how to act like a gentleman.* "Lily, I need to talk to– "

"Damn, girl, when you trade up, you really trade up." Amara had followed us and stared at me appraisingly. At any other time, I may have been interested. She was beautiful in an exotic way, with firm tits and legs that went on for miles. She also had a look on her face that suggested she wanted to eat me alive. That had never interested me. I'd always preferred a challenge. Lily challenged me. I had no idea what drew me to her like this, what bond may have formed from our ordeal, but the more I thought about it, the more I wanted to see it through. I didn't have any idea how things could work out, but nothing ventured, nothing gained, right?

"Amara, stop." Lily's stance on the chair was rigid, unhappy.

Amara waved her away. "Just kidding around, Lily. Don't be so serious all the time. Look around you. All these people came to the club to have a good time. You're free of Michael, finally. You should loosen up. Look at Xander; he wants to have a good time." She winked. "I can tell."

"As a matter of fact…" I grinned at the two of them and gestured to the bartender. "Drinks are on me," I told her. "Whatever these two want."

"Oh, just one, then," Amara said. "Tequila shots!"

"Amara," Lily scolded, "you're supposed to be the designated driver!"

"It's just one. Don't be a spoilsport."

I leaned close to Lily's ear. "Come back with me," I urged, my voice a whisper. The bartender placed the drinks on the bar in front of the ladies. I hadn't ordered another. I planned to leave soon.

Lily shook her head and turned back to her friend. She held up a single finger and glared. "*One*, Amara. I want to get home safely. I'm going to the ladies' room."

Lily jumped up and whirled on me when I grabbed her wrist, gesturing to her drink with my chin, a challenge in my eyes.

"*You* drink it. *I* don't want anything." She stormed away.

Amara slid onto Lily's stool and smiled up at me through her long lashes. "She wasn't like that when we got here. Not sure what's going on with her. You know, Xander, I've always been a big fan. I've watched every meet they've shown on TV." She ran her hand along my bicep. "You seem much more … I don't know, approachable in person.

And strong. The camera doesn't do you justice. Or maybe there's just something about being able to run my hand… up and down…"

I grabbed hold of her hand and removed it. "Too God damned easy. I have a hard time believing this act works on anyone. Listen, since you're supposedly the designated driver, I'm going to assume you came in one car."

"Who the hell are you calling easy?"

I raised my eyebrows and looked pointedly at my arm. "I don't want you getting drunk tonight. Or, if you do, call a cab. I'm going to take Lily home myself."

"She seems pretty pissed. I'm not sure you'll have a shot with her."

I rose from my barstool. "Be safe tonight." I took off in the direction of the restrooms.

There was no sign of Lily, so I assumed she must still be inside. A payphone had been placed in a darkened corner near the restrooms, so I went and sat on the stool to wait. Why would this bar have a payphone? Everything in here was modern and streamlined, yet they had this relic here. In this age, everyone has cell phones anyway, and if they were too drunk to figure it out, the bartender would undoubtedly call a cab for the patron. Why the payphone, then?

I considered barging into the restroom and dragging her out, but the steady stream of women walking in and out deterred me. I could just imagine them beating me with their purses and security dragging me out. *Patience, Xander.*

Amara was right. Lily *did* seem pissed. Maybe I should have stuck around and asked her some more questions. What had I done? She'd seemed receptive toward seeing me when I approached her on the dance floor. So many questions flashed through my head. I still didn't understand why she'd agreed to come back here or, for that matter, why *I'd* come back here. I should have just called her up and forgotten about being a vigilante or about finding a random hookup.

Lily finally emerged from the bathroom. I rose to my feet and stepped behind her, jerking her into the corner. I pulled her body flush against mine, her back to my front.

"Have I done something to upset you?" I breathed into her ear, my voice raspy.

"Leave me alone."

"No. I can't." I suckled her earlobe, my teeth grazing her skin. I heard her breath catch. *Good.*

She turned in my arms to look up at me. "Why don't you and Amara just go have fun together?"

I gripped her arm tighter, my other hand snaking around to hug her belly. "You can't be serious."

"I saw the way you two were looking at each other. She was throwing herself at you, and you didn't mind at all."

"You saw nothing, because there wasn't anything to see."

She thrashed. "You're just as bad as Michael, and she is supposed to be my friend. Just like Allison. I can't go through this again! Let me go."

"Lily. Calm down. She tripped. I caught her. I'll admit she was being a little… obvious in her flirtation, but I never showed her any interest. It's only you."

Lily continued to squirm. I gripped both of her forearms and spun her around to face me. "Lily, please hear me out." She shook her head. "Listen to me. I'm not going to lie to you. I can't stop thinking about you. I came here tonight intending to pick up someone random to take my mind off you, but it wasn't working. No one in this entire club could measure up. Lily, I can't promise you forever. I can't even promise you a week. I've never been the type to settle down. What I can promise you is that right here, right now, my every thought is of *you*."

Lily looked to be in a trance, but she quickly shook herself out of it. "I knew you didn't come here for me, like you said."

"Ah, but I might as well have. None of them stood out to me. Not one. I turned Amara down. As forward as she is, she can't hold a candle to you. Come back with me. We'll take things one day at a time and see how we feel."

She hesitated, so I squeezed her arms and pulled her closer. "Come with me," I breathed against her mouth, then I sealed the deal with a gentle kiss. "Please."

Lily smiled against my lips. "Yes."

I tightened my arms around her, deepening the kiss. I thrust my tongue into her mouth to tangle with hers. She placed her hand on my chest and groaned.

I broke away. "Come with me." I led her by the hand out the nearby back door into a side alley and was relieved to see no one there.

"Is it safe here?" Lily asked. She sounded nervous, but her eyes glinted with excitement and desire.

I pulled her past some empty beer crates and shoved her against the brick wall, careful to cushion her head with my hand. "Probably not. We'll have to be fast. I need you, Lily. I don't want to wait anymore."

At her nod, I reached into my pocket and drew out a condom. The crinkle of the wrapper sounded louder than normal in the silence of the alley. Unwilling to waste another moment, I unfastened my jeans and slid it on. Her chocolate eyes were pools of blackness in the poor lighting, but there was no mistaking the need I could see there. I'd already had her today, but it wasn't enough–for either of us. In that moment, I wasn't sure it would ever be enough.

I reached under her skirt to slide her panties out of the way and was thrilled to discover the slender string of a thong. I inhaled sharply when I felt that she was already soaking wet for me. "Lily," I rasped, "I want to remove these with my teeth later."

"Yesss."

"Put your legs around me. This is going to be hard and fast. I don't know how much time we have." I placed my hands under her firm ass and lifted. She wrapped her arms and legs around me, and I impaled her in one fierce move. We had none of the awkwardness of a couple getting to know how to be with each other. We fit together perfectly.

I thrust my cock into her, using the wall to help support her. I was drunk from the taste of her lips on mine, by her smell, the feel of her juices rubbing all over my balls. I'd had great sex before, but never like this.

"Shit, Xander, harder. Please," she moaned.

Around the corner, I heard the back door of the club swing open. I froze in place and covered Lily's mouth with my hand. "Shhh…"

The empty crates did a good job of shielding us from view if anyone happened to look in our direction. Even so, it was best to not draw their attention. With a wicked grin, I pumped into her without a sound. I released her mouth and shifted her weight so that I could angle myself better. My breath caught when she wrapped her arms tighter around me and bit down hard on my shoulder.

"Hold the door for me, would ya?" came a deep voice from around the corner. "That door shuts and we'll have a bitch of a time getting back in. The lines for this place are ridiculous. Damn. I lost my lighter."

"I've got mine," another voice answered. "Good thing the chicks here are hot. Otherwise there'd be no point to this place."

"Speaking of, did you see the hot blonde in the miniskirt? She came in with that Indian chick you were talking to for so long, but she vanished into the bathroom a while ago. Too bad. I bet those legs of hers would look real good around my waist."

I growled low in my throat and continued to thrust into Lily. She tried to smother her gasp in my throat. "Wait, Xander," she whispered urgently. "Oh my God, please wait. I'm getting close. They're right *here*."

I squeezed my hand between us to find her clit and rubbed it with firm strokes that matched my steady rhythm. She clamped her eyes shut and bit down hard on her lower lip, her breath loud and heavy through her nose. Her pussy clenched tightly around me as if that would stop me, but it only served to spur me on.

"I don't think Amara is Indian, man," continued the second voice.

"Does it matter?"

"I guess not. Won't make a bit of difference in the morning."

Lily whimpered and bit me again. I grunted as the sharp, delicious pain flooded my system. Her cunt began to pulse all around me, her nails pressed into my back. Her orgasm triggered my own release, and I buried myself as far inside her as I could, stifling a moan.

"Hey, did you hear that?" asked the first guy.

"Probably a stray cat. Will you hurry it up already? I already finished my cigarette. I want to get back in there."

"Just a minute. It didn't sound like any cat I've ever heard. Came from down that alley."

I slowly withdrew, releasing her legs so she could stand on her own. I caressed her cheek and grinned, holding my index finger up to my lips.

"Man, who cares? I'm going back in. You can look for your phantom animal by yourself. I'm interested in a different kind of pussy."

"All right, all right. You win. Let's go back. Maybe your girl's friend is back, anyway." A moment later, the sound of the door slamming filled the air.

We both exhaled as one. I chuckled. "I thought that guy was going to come find us for sure."

"You're impossible," she scolded.

"For you, I'm easy. Let's get out of here."

Lily chewed her lip, her brow furrowed. "I should go find Amara. Tell her where I'm going."

"I already told her you'd catch a ride with me. Besides, you heard those guys talking. One of them apparently hooked up with Amara the instant I stepped away, and the other is looking for you."

She chuckled. "Then you'll just have to stay close by me so he doesn't get near."

"Why?"

"Why what?"

"Why do you want to go back in there? Like I already said, I told Amara I would bring you home. Just text her if you want."

Lily frowned. "I guess you're right. Those guys were right about the line for this place, too. Amara and I had to wait for half an hour, and I know some had to wait even longer." She smoothed out her skirt and adjusted her shirt, momentarily exposing her tits. "It's a shame, though."

I stared at her chest, transfixed. "Why is that?"

She laughed. "Hey, my eyes are up here." She gave me a quick peck on my mouth. "I don't know. I just have a bad feeling. I'm going to worry all night."

Well, hell. I can't have that. "All right. We'll go in for just a minute. Say what you want, then we'll go. Okay?"

"No, Xander, it's okay. I'll *try* not to think about it." By her tone, I could tell that this was the same type of situation as when a woman said she was *fine*. She said it, but she didn't mean it. No way was I falling for *that*.

"No. Let's go find your friend." My voice was deeper than I meant it to be, a command that allowed for no disagreement. I took her hand and pulled her around the front of the building, ignoring the massive crowd of people gathered

95

outside. I led her straight to the bouncer, who leaned against the wall, smoking.

He pushed away from the wall to remove the rope that was such a meager barrier blocking those outside. I slipped him another fifty as we passed him.

"Is that really all we had to do? Bribe him? And we wouldn't have had to wait outside in high heels?"

I chuckled and squeezed her hand, leaning toward her to talk close to her ear. "Doubtful. I didn't bribe him, I tipped him. He always lets me in straight away. *You* could have bypassed the line by simply showing off your… assets." I laughed when she smacked me on the arm. "Come on, let's find your friend."

We checked out the bar area, since that was the last place we'd seen Amara. Scanning the area, we started to turn back to the dance floor, when I caught sight of the bartender signaling to me. Still holding Lily's hand, I started to head that way, only to feel her jerk away from me. I turned to look at her.

"There she is!" Lily took off onto the dance floor. I wanted to stop her, but the look on Chrissy's face told me I'd better see what she wanted. I focused on the direction Lily ran, then marched to the bar.

"What's up?"

"That guy you were looking for was here."

"Oh?"

"Yup. Strangest thing. He approached your girl's friend, but ran off in a hurry when two other guys came in from smoking and joined them."

"Did he leave?"

"I'm not sure. What do you need with him, anyway?" Her wide eyes sparkled in the reflected light from the strobes on the nearby dance floor.

"Just between us?"

She smirked and leaned forward, displaying her cleavage. "Of course."

"Keep an eye on him if you see him again. I think he may be spiking drinks."

"Wait, what? I'll call the cops if I see him again."

"No, Chrissy. I have no solid proof it was him. If anything, seeing cops will probably tip him off and he'll move on. Just watch out for him for now, okay?"

Her forehead wrinkled as she considered my words. "At least he wouldn't be here anymore. I don't see how that's not an improvement."

"Short term, yes. Long term, wouldn't it be better to catch him in the act here, where we're on to his tricks?"

"I don't like this."

"I don't like getting tangled up in all of this, either. Still…" I trailed off, lost in thought.

"This have anything to do with the fact that you've now been seen here with that girl twice? I thought the day would never come."

"First time for everything, Chrissy. Keep an eye out. I'm going to go find Lily."

I stepped onto the dance floor and searched for Lily but couldn't find her. I was so intent I almost missed seeing Amara and nearly walked right past, only noticing her at the last second. She was dancing with some guy I'd never seen before, grinding up against him. As I watched, she tossed her hair to the side and bared her neck. He was quick to move in and kiss her there, his attention quite obviously down her shirt.

"Hey, Amara, did Lily find you?"

The guy jerked away, an annoyed look on his face. I stood up straighter, displaying that I wasn't intimidated. Amara grinned at me, flashing her white teeth. "Xander, I didn't expect to see you again tonight. Dance with us."

I glanced at the guy she was with, and it was all I could do not to roll my eyes. "Amara, focus. Where is Lily?"

She pointed. "I'll still be here when you change your mind." She started to turn back to her date, but I gripped her wrist, squeezing tightly and pulling her close enough to smell her perfume.

"Hey!" the guy yelled. I glared and held up my index finger in the universal gesture for "wait one moment" and hoped he would back off.

"I don't know what your problem is, but this," I gestured between us, "isn't attractive. I'm interested in Lily, and as her friend you should be happy for her. I'm sure this guy you're dancing with isn't impressed by you throwing yourself at me."

She jerked her wrist, and I let her go. "Throwing myself at you? You have some nerve."

"Right. Whatever. I'm going to find Lily."

I looked in the direction Amara had indicated and found myself locked in Lily's dark gaze. Damn, she looked angry. She turned to a guy who stood nearby and beckoned to him. In a flash she had spun him around and pulled his face down so she could kiss him. Her head cocked to the side and she glared daggers at me.

I wasn't stupid. I knew what she was doing. I wasn't going to take the bait. I watched the guy pull her close, saw her shirt bunch, and realized he was touching her naked back.

Before I even fully realized what was happening, I had marched over to them and hauled him off her. It wasn't until I felt the pain in my right hand that I realized I had punched him in the face.

Oh shit. God damn it, what have I done?

The dancers who had been gyrating and grinding on the floor all stopped and stared. The guy gripped his nose, trying to stem the flow of blood as he struggled to his feet. I had to get out of there.

The first camera flash went off. I wasn't sure if it was directed at the man on the floor or at me. More followed soon after. I grabbed Lily by the elbow and steered her out of the building, signaling for the valet.

"Let me go!" she snarled. "Let me go or I'll scream."

"We need to talk. We were *supposed* to talk, but instead you decided to put on some insane show for the club. Childish. Almost as childish as my fucking reaction. I need to get out of here. I can't stay and wait for that guy to realize who I am and call the cops. Plus, people are taking pictures. I need you to come with me."

The valet brought my car around. I opened up the passenger door, then walked around to the driver side. "Come on, Lily. Hear me out. I promise I'll take you home if that's what you want. Please."

She stood there and stared at me. I sighed, preparing to go grab the door and leave without her.

"Get in the car, Lily. Unless you'd rather be part of the circus that may or may not be happening in there now."

She hesitated a moment more, chewing on her lower lip. Then, finally, she lowered herself into the car and buckled up.

Without another word, I took off, heading northeast on Interstate-4.

"Where are we going?" We had made it several miles up the road and would soon be outside the main part of Orlando.

I glanced at her out of the corner of my eye. I knew we needed to talk, but I had no idea what I wanted to say. "I'm just driving. Where would you like to go?"

"Take me home, then," she mumbled.

I nodded, but made no move to change course. "Lily?"

"What?"

"What the hell was that back there?"

"You're one to talk."

I ran my left hand through my light brown hair and counted to ten. This chick would be the death of me. Was sex with her really that good to warrant me dealing with this? "What are you talking about?"

"I saw you with Amara, practically letting her eat out of the palm of your hand. You're just like Michael."

I put on my hazards and pulled over to the shoulder. I continued to stare straight ahead. "First of all, I'm not convinced that girl is your friend. What you saw was me having words with her for the way she was disrespecting you. Second of all, what the hell is with all these people? Between one hooking up with your ex and Amara throwing herself at me when she *knew* we were together, I'm at a loss for words. With friends like them, you don't need enemies."

She leaned her arm against the window and cupped her forehead in her hand. "Were we, though?"

"Were we what?"

"Together?"

I resisted the urge to rub my temples. "Lily, we had *just* fucked in a filthy back alley. Not sure how much more together we could have been tonight!"

Maybe this was all a mistake. No matter what chemistry I felt with her, it didn't change the fact that she had some serious baggage. Her display at the club proved that she was bad for me, bad for my public image. I gave into the urge and rubbed my temples, pressing my head back into the headrest as I realized that there had been at least *two* tabloid reporters in that club tonight, and both of them knew who I was.

"I'm sorry, Xander," she said in a small voice. "I screwed up. I guess I just don't understand how someone like you could possibly want anything to do with me."

"*I* don't understand why you're confused by that. Look at you. Wearing that cock-teasing mini skirt and tank top. Those heels that make your legs look like they go on for days. Your deep brown eyes that can make a man want to be a better person, make *me* think about changing for you..." I stopped short as I realized I'd overshared. "... I wasn't the only one staring at you in there, you know."

"I just didn't expect any of this. Michael and I just broken up, and now here you are, and you're so intense I got sucked in. I've a weird feeling I haven't even touched the tip of the iceberg on how intense being with you is. If we were to even *try* being a couple, I'm sure I'd have to deal with competitions, and practices, and—"

"Image."

"Yes. Wait, image?"

"Yes. Every single thing I do has to have my image in mind. You know how it is. You're in this business. The world is just waiting for me to fuck up so they can all point and laugh. I may not be a huge movie star, but I'm still in the public eye, and my little stunt tonight was bad. I'm going to be eaten alive." I looked at my hand. The skin was split on two of my knuckles, and dried blood caked the back of my hand. I flexed my fingers and winced.

"I won't let that happen."

"You can't stop it. Even though I don't believe you'd write the story, nothing is stopping Amara. We didn't exactly part on the best terms tonight. Besides, I saw flashes going off. It's only a matter of time before I'm recognized and someone sells their picture to the highest bidder. Only a matter of time before that guy realizes he can sue me. Do you even know who he was?"

Lily shook her head. "No. Just some guy who hit on me. Probably the one who almost caught us in the alley."

"Awesome."

"I'll talk to Amara. I don't doubt she'll bring his friend home with her, so I'll catch her for breakfast around the crack of noon."

"Just leave it. Fat chance of her not wanting to bring in that story. She'll be all over it. Don't add fuel to the fire."

"But—"

"I said leave it, Lily." My Mustang shook as cars flew past on my side. I knew we should get a move on soon, but the tension between us was still so thick it was almost palpable.

"Fine." Her voice was barely above a whisper again. "What was it you wanted to say earlier, anyway? You were so adamant we needed to talk."

I shrugged. "I wanted to talk about you coming back to my place."

"And then what?"

"What kind of a question is that? We unwind. Have some fun together."

"Until when?"

"What?"

"So I come over tonight and go home when? Later tonight? Tomorrow? Then what? Is that it?"

"Like I told you in the club, Lily, I can't promise forever. I can't even promise next week. Will you be able to live with that?"

"I don't know." She chewed her lip.

"But in a traditional relationship, isn't that normal? A couple gets together and tries to make it work. Either it works out and they stay together, or it doesn't and they break up. I can't think of too many couples that just decide on forever the first time they meet."

She paused. "True enough, I guess. But it just feels like we're going into this expecting it to fail.

What's the point of even trying when you can't even commit to the *possibility* of a relationship? It feels like a waste of time, no matter how incredible the sex is."

I grinned. "It is pretty incredible, isn't it?"

She smacked me on the upper arm and laughed. "Focus, Xander!"

"I am focused. Focused on how hot you are. Come on, Lily. We could be good together. Let's just see how things go. Besides, that tiny little skirt and tank top would look stunning on the floor next to my bed."

She giggled, a beautiful sound that sent my pulse racing. "You're impossible."

I reached forward and traced her lower lip with my thumb. "I already told you, for you, I am easy. So where are we going?"

She shook her head. "Not my place. Let's go back to yours."

"Your wish is my command." I put the car in gear and merged into traffic.

CHAPTER NINE

"So what's the plan?" Lily asked.

"Always looking for a plan. I have none, just winging it. Are you hungry?" I wandered into the kitchen and rifled through the fridge.

"Not really. We had dinner before heading to the club."

I grabbed a bottle of wine, two glasses, and a can of cashews. "I don't think you've seen my bedroom yet."

"The room we slept in last night isn't your bedroom?"

"Guest room. It almost never gets used. Come on up." I gestured for her to precede me up the stairs.

She snickered. "You just want to stare at my ass while I can't stop you."

"It's a fine ass, for sure. Regardless, it's good manners to allow the lady to go up the stairs first."

She paused, staring at me. "Are you for real?"

"What?"

"You claim you've never had a real, meaningful relationship, yet you always open doors, and now this stair thing. Something doesn't add up."

"My mother taught me how to behave. That's all. Stop overthinking it."

She hesitated a moment longer, then climbed the stairs. I followed, happily watching the swish of her short skirt as it swayed and getting a peek at what was hidden beneath. Acting like a gentleman did have its advantages.

Lily paused on the landing, hesitant to walk through the open door into my room first, I supposed. I pretended not to notice she had stopped walking so I could "accidentally" bump into her and wrap my arms around her stomach. Taking a deep, obvious breath, I reveled in her scent. Sex and lavender; it was a heady smell that brought me back to our alley tryst. With regret, I withdrew from around her, careful not to drop the wine or glasses.

"Sorry," I murmured in her ear. "After you."

My bedroom was the nicest room in the house, aside from my home gym. A large sleigh bed with a black leather headboard dominated the open space. A desk lined one wall, and a dresser sat against another. There was an oversized walk-in closet and, through the open door near the dresser, a private bathroom with an oversized shower and hot tub.

I set the glasses on the desk and flipped on the light. I watched Lily look around the room as I poured the wine and took a sip, letting the flavors roll over my tongue. Satisfied, I handed her the other glass, watching the way her throat moved when she swallowed.

I set the glass down with a *clink*. "Cards?"

"Excuse me?"

"Do you play cards?"

"Not often." Lily looked completely bewildered. I popped the lid off the cashews and smirked. "Why are we playing cards?"

"I think strip poker sounds fun."

"You *would* think that."

"I'm usually right."

"Okay, so if you win, you get to see me naked. If I win, what?"

"You mean you don't want to see me naked?" Silence was my only answer. I chuckled. "All right, Lily, what do you want if you win?"

"Information."

"You can ask me anything; you should know that." I was genuinely confused at her request. It's not like I was hiding things.

"Sure. I ask, and you always deflect or distract me. I want you to answer anything, and answer honestly."

I hesitated. Something about her tone gave me pause. She was up to something… still, I was confident in my card playing ability.

"Agreed, but let's sweeten it further. Whoever loses the round can choose their fate. She can remove any article of clothing, answer a question with absolute honesty, *or* must perform a task left to my imagination."

"She? Your imagination? Kind of cocky, aren't you?"

"Do we have a deal?"

She thought for a moment. "What kind of tasks? Cleaning? Sexual?"

"Anything."

Lily narrowed her eyes. "Make it two things. And winner's choice, not loser's."

"In a hurry to get naked for me? Or you want to see how devious I can be in regard to tasks?"

"Neither. I plan to win. I have a lot of questions."

I considered. Two "prizes" would speed things to their inevitable conclusion, *but* this game was all about seduction. I wanted to drive her wild for me. Stalling for time, I popped more cashews in my mouth.

Perhaps this would work after all. I'd twist it so I could see what sort of things she wanted done to *herself,* as well. Plus that would limit the number of nosy questions. Even though I was pretty open about things, I shouldn't lose sight of what she does for a living. "Done. Two things, but the winner chooses one, and the loser chooses one to have happen to her."

"Do they teach this level of cockiness in some school somewhere? I mean, I'd bet you couldn't lay it on any thicker if you tried. No deal. The point of two prizes was for me to ask you questions."

"Then you'll just need to win. What's the matter? Afraid you won't be able to?"

She gulped down the rest of her wine. "Oh, fine. Get the damned cards."

"Wait here." I left the room and walked down the stairs again, wincing at the ache in my ankle. I went into the closet of the guest room and pulled out a collapsible card table and a folding chair, then grabbed the cards. The nauseating smell from our disastrous night together still permeated the room. I should have cleaned it earlier. I firmly closed the door as if that would make it all go away and returned to Lily.

"Wow, a card table and everything? You do this often?"

"No, not often at all. I can't remember the last time I played cards with anyone." That wasn't exactly the truth. I had played with my buddy John, Sam, and his wife Melissa quite a few times in the past. It had been a while, though, and I knew she was asking if I often played strip poker with other women.

I finished setting up the table and chair, then spun my padded desk chair over to the table as well. I refilled the wine glasses and shuffled. "Five card draw. No wild cards. That okay with you?"

"Umm... sure."

Oh, this was going to be all too easy.

I dealt, leaving my hand on the table while I watched her. She picked them up and rearranged them in her hand, her delicate fingers awkwardly moving cards around as if she'd never seen them before. Her confident bravado she'd displayed during "negotiations" had completely vanished.

Her nostrils flared; it was adorable. The frown line on her forehead relaxed a little. She placed two cards on the table and tapped them with her nails.

"Two, please."

Without looking away, I dealt her two more. Her eyes widened and darted to mine. She had a shitty poker face, it was almost comical. Whatever she had must be pretty good.

"Xander, aren't you going to look at yours?"

I gave her a crooked half-smile and picked up my cards. I had decided that, no matter what, I was going to throw this hand. I discarded two queens and a ten, drawing three new ones. I set them down and took a sip of wine. "Staying in or folding?"

"Oh, I'm in," she answered a little too quickly. She was trying and failing to hide her excitement.

I toyed with my glass. "So am I. Call."

She flipped her cards over, practically giddy in her perceived victory. "Full house. Read 'em and weep."

"Full house, huh? You hustling me, Lily?"

"What? Did I say it wrong? That's what they say in the movies," she said with a giggle.

"Well, you got me. I have a pair of nines."

"You lose! What are you going to do now, Xander?" She rubbed her hands together, a wicked look on her face.

"Hmmm." I untied my tie and tossed it onto the bed. "Just as well. I only left that thing on since we were playing strip poker. Much more comfortable now."

"I'm glad to hear that. Wouldn't want you to be uncomfortable. Well, not physically. Now it's question time!" She rubbed her hands together, an evil grin plastered on her face. "Hmm… I'd better make it good. What should I ask?"

"Is that your question?"

"You should be so lucky. I'm thinking out loud, that's all. I want to choose the right one. I want to ask you why you don't have girlfriends. I want to know how many women you've been with, how old you were the first time. I want… wait, I know." She paused, her forehead wrinkling. "Why me?"

"Why you?"

"Yes. That's my question. You could have had any girl in that club. But you took me home. Why?"

I drew out finishing my wine and refilling it, buying time. "Like I told you yesterday, you stood out to me. I wanted you from the moment I saw you. As for tonight, I don't know, Lily. You've gotten under my skin. Maybe it's what we went through, maybe it's fate, but I feel drawn to you. When you aren't around, I miss you. I couldn't stop thinking of you after I dropped you off this afternoon. And, then, when you are around, I want nothing more than to be inside you. It's you because I can't seem to help myself, and that is the whole truth. Is it my shuffle?"

"Don't change the subject, Xander. I still want to know why. The *real* reason why."

I picked up the cards and straightened them, feeling frustrated. I didn't know how to explain better because I didn't understand myself. "That makes two of us, Lily. I don't know what more to tell you."

Lily took the cards from me, shuffled, and dealt. Compared to the last time, she had very little reaction. A glance at my hand showed me the three of spades, and a three, four, five, and an ace–all of hearts. Why had I said no wild cards? Oh well. Chances of getting a two when I discarded a single card was pretty remote, but I needed to decide to try for the last heart or to play off the low pair. I smiled at Lily and dropped a single card. "One, please."

She handed me a card, then discarded three of her own. The new card was the ten of diamonds. I had nothing. I set all my cards down. "I'm in."

Lily's eyes searched mine. "I fold." Her voice was so small I almost questioned hearing it.

"What was that? Sounded like you folded. You know what that means…"

"It means we deal the next round?"

"Nice try. It means you lose. So what's it gonna be?"

"Ask me a question."

I stilled. It hadn't occurred to me that she'd want me to ask her things. I felt confused and unprepared. What was this, anyway? Some odd variant of *Truth or Dare*? Why had I even agreed? We should have stuck with tasks and nudity.

"That's not what I had in mind."

"Well, you shot down my idea of both prizes being the winner's choice, so deal with it. What's your question?"

I'd show her. She wanted to play *Truth or Dare*? So be it. "Fine. What is your deepest, darkest sexual fantasy?"

Lily's complexion paled. "What kind of question is that? I have no idea."

"I'm waiting."

She picked at the vinyl table covering with a scarlet fingernail. I sat back in my chair, steepling my fingers in front of me.

"Well, promise not to laugh?"

"How can I promise something without knowing exactly what I'm promising? I promise to *try* not to laugh."

"Damn you. Fine. We did it tonight."

I leaned forward, regarding her. "Go on."

"In the alley. It was so… forbidden, so sexy. We could have been caught at any moment. The risk turned me on."

"Why would I laugh at that?"

"I don't know. Because you're *you*. Because you'd think I meant that you're my…"

"Yes?"

"Nope. I'm done there. Your turn to choose something I have to do."

"I'd think you meant I'm your–what?" It hit me. "Your fantasy?"

"No! That's not what I said," she squealed. "Fuck you, Xander."

"That's the plan for later. For now, take something off."

Leaning forward, Lily slid her hand under the back of her shirt, lifting the front just enough to yank out a strapless black bra. She tossed it on the bed. "Now *I'm* more comfortable." Her tone sounded exactly as mine had when discussing my tie. I stared at her chest, admiring the way her nipples pressed against the thin fabric of her tank top. "Less staring, more dealing."

I chuckled and grabbed the cards. It was on now. I quickly shuffled and dealt, keeping an eye on her and watching for her tells. I won the next round with three of a kind, barely beating her two pair. She chose to remove her earrings, then looked up at me expectantly.

"I think I'll go with a task this time," I said at length. My mind raced as I considered the possibilities. The thought that overrode the rest, though, was I wanted an unobstructed view of her beautiful breasts. "Take off your shirt," I bit out, already turned on from just imagining what I had in store for her.

"That's not how this is supposed to work. I'm supposed to get to choose what clothing I take off and when."

"That would be true had I told you to remove some of your clothes. I didn't. You are fulfilling a task. Now, do what I told you."

Lily took on a stubborn stance and looked like she wanted to argue. I leaned forward in my chair, folding my arms on the card table in front of me. I tapped my fingers impatiently as I stared her down. She swallowed hard, then shook her head and sighed. "Fine." She snatched off her tank top and flung it over her shoulder.

My eyes devoured her chest. Her nipples stood erect, begging me to touch them. Outwardly, I maintained my composure, not moving, forcing myself to breathe normally. In my head, however, I was feasting on those nipples, her back arched as she moaned, begging me to touch even more. *Fuck me.* My heart rate accelerated, my dick pressed painfully against my pants. I wanted to adjust myself, needed to adjust myself, but refused to let her see how much she affected me. I'd only had her a short time ago, but already needed her again. I forced my eyes up to hers, noticing her eyes had darkened. Oh, yeah. She wanted me every bit as much as I wanted her.

I cleared my throat, forcing our attention back to the game. At least I tried to. She dealt, but I couldn't focus. While we examined our cards, I sneakily reached under the table and adjusted my dick.

Lily was terrible at bluffing. When I met her gaze, I saw the excitement there as obvious as if someone had written "I have a winning hand" on her forehead. A quick glance at my cards told me I didn't have a chance in hell. I discarded three, but the new ones were not any better.

"I'm out. You want me to take off my pants, right?"

"Wrong! Question time. How many women have you been with?"

Well, doesn't that *just destroy the mood?* I frowned. "I don't know."

"You said you'd answer honestly."

"And I did." I unbuttoned my shirt and tossed it behind me on the bed, then grabbed the cards.

"Wait. How was that honest? You must have some idea. Example: I've been with five different men."

I sighed, shuffling the cards absently. "I was with five women in just the last couple of weeks. More than five, now that I think about it. I said I don't know because I don't know. You're a reporter, Lily. A tabloid reporter. I'm having trouble with the idea that you didn't know that."

"So when you saw me in the club, you'd just intended me to be a one night fling for you?"

"Yes. Yet, here we are, together on an entirely different day. Until *this* question, I was having a good time. I told you I wanted to see you again, told you I couldn't stop thinking about you. Why isn't that enough? Can't it be enough for now? We'll see how things go, like regular people." I really regretting agreeing to answer her questions. Nothing good could come of this.

"Yes, Xander. I'm sorry."

"Besides, those were *two* questions." I grinned, making a show out of checking out her bare tits. I wanted to lighten the mood and regain some of the sexual tension that had been building between us. This game needed to be put back on track.

I won the next hand. Lily shimmied out of her skirt and stood before me in nothing but a tiny black thong and high heels. I swallowed hard, my mouth going dry. All my annoyance from just a few minutes before evaporated. Christ, she was hot.

"What do you want me to do now, Xander?"

"I–" I cleared my throat and tried again. "I want you to kneel down on the floor next to me."

"What? Why? Are we done playing cards?"

"Why isn't part of the deal. Just do it."

Lily circled the table and dropped to her knees at my side. Her tits hung freely, her nipples were hard, pointed. I wanted to touch them. My mouth watered at the thought of taking them in my mouth.

"Now what?"

"Lean forward. More, a little more. Yes, just like that. Now look at me." Her eyes rose to meet mine. Her eyes were dark with desire, her breasts thrust forward, begging for attention. "Do you know how sexy you are, kneeling there in nothing but your heels and thong? I want so badly to touch you."

"Then do it." She breathed heavily.

I flashed her a wicked grin. "Not yet. First, I want *you* to touch yourself. "Feel your breasts, caress them, massage them. Let me see how much you enjoy it."

"I'd enjoy it more if you did it for me."

"Soon. Very soon. But not yet. Go on; I'm waiting." She ran her palms over her thighs and up to her belly. She hesitated, tensing. "Close your eyes. Don't think about being watched. Pretend your hands are *my* hands. Pleasure yourself the way I would pleasure you."

She closed her eyes and threw her head back. Her hands skated up her skin, testing the weight of her breasts. She pinched her nipples, her breath coming faster.

I fell silent, watching her in rapt attention. She squeezed her tits together, releasing rhythmically, kneading her flesh. My hands twitched, I wanted so badly to join her. She pinched her nipples again and moaned. The sound awoke every nerve in my body.

CHAPTER NINE

"Happy now?" she asked, opening her eyes. I watched her gaze travel to my crotch, my tented pants more than obvious. She licked her lips, her expression predatory. She looked like she wanted to eat me alive.

I held out my hand, refusing to give in, determined to remain in control. "Almost. Suck it."

She eagerly rose up on her knees and moved toward my lap, but I stopped her, restraining her with the hand I had offered. I traced her lower lip with my thumb. "This. Suck *this.*"

With agonizing slowness, Lily drew my thumb into her mouth. Her eyes locked with mine. She swirled her tongue around, sucking hard. She scraped her teeth across the skin and moaned as if my thumb were a delicacy.

My cock throbbed at the sound. I couldn't take it anymore. I needed her badly, needed to sink balls-deep inside her. The only thing stopping me was my own iron will. I was determined to play out this game of seduction, though it would inevitably drive me insane. My breath caught as she drew my thumb fully into her mouth. *Oh, fuck!* Why hadn't I taken my pants off earlier when I had the chance? They felt much too tight. Gently I pulled away from her. "Lily…"

"Yes?" Her voice was breathy, full of need.

"It's your shuffle."

Confused, she jumped to her feet and plopped into the chair. She dealt the cards, which I tried to focus on, but all I could think about was getting her lips wrapped around my cock. Feeling her lick the bead of pre-come off the tip and taking me all the way back into her throat. I managed to pull off a single pair, which was mostly by sheer chance. She won the hand.

"Wait." Lily chewed her lip.

"What?"

"It's just… I want to ask you a question, but there's something I'd like you to do." She looked up at me pleadingly. Did she expect me to let her do both? Not a chance. These pants were coming off.

"You'll have to choose, Lily." I rose to my feet and shoved my pants off, kicking off my shoes as well.

"Technically, that's *two* articles of clothing," Lily said, her eyes travelling down my chest to fixate on the bulge in my boxers.

"Forget the shoes, they were in my way. What's your question?"

"Not a question this time." Lily stood up and faced me, shameless. "In the alley, you said you wanted to pull this thong off me using only your teeth. Do it."

"With pleasure." This game had been meant to seduce Lily, but it was quickly backfiring on me. Two steps brought me to her. I passionately kissed her, pressing my dick into her stomach and letting her feel how hard she'd made me. I shoved my tongue into her mouth, possessing her as much as I could. My hands gripped her hair, my fingers moving restlessly. I started to drop to my knees in front of her when she slipped her hand into the hole of my boxers and gripped my shaft.

I let out a strangled gasp and broke away, breathing heavily. Her fingers squeezed me, sliding up toward the tip. My hips pressed forward of their own volition.

"Stop." I bit the word out as if it pained me. In a way, it had. Her touch where I wanted it most was my undoing. I needed her now. I was so hard it was amazing I had any blood left to allow my brain to function at all, as hard as I'd ever been. Maybe more so. No more games. Fuck poker. I was going to poke *her*.

"Are you sure?"

"No. I want…" I dug deep and forced my body to relax. Gently, I removed her hand and dropped to my knees. "I believe you asked me to do something."

I could smell her arousal, and *God* was it sexy. I slowly rubbed her legs with my hands so she could feel the rough calluses running up and down. Slipping my tongue under the thin strap of her thong over her hip, I drew it into my mouth and gripped it with my teeth and dragged it down. I kissed my way across her belly, delighting in the way her skin twitched and how she trembled as I went, then tugged on the other side.

"Jesus Christ… I can't fucking help myself around you." I yanked her thong down with my hands, steadying her as I pulled them over her left leg. I squeezed my torso between her legs and balanced the left one over my shoulder.

"That wasn't your teeth," she gasped.

"You'll just have to deal with the fact that I can't resist getting at least a little taste of your sweet pussy."

My tongue licked her sopping wet entrance and stroked upward toward her clit. I gripped her hips to steady her as I plunged my tongue inside. The flavor of her sweet juices seduced my tongue, urged me to consume her.

"Oh, God, Xander. Fuck me, please. Now. I need your cock." I couldn't answer; my mouth was otherwise occupied. I wanted her to come, wanted her juices to coat my tongue, to feel her grind her body on my face. I moaned into her pussy and dug my fingers into her ass cheeks. I fucked her relentlessly with my tongue, loving the way she shook, loving the sounds she made. She was delicious, like a fine wine.

My tongue moved to flick her clit as I eased two fingers into her swollen pussy and curled them inside her to reach her g-spot. She gasped and bucked her hips, riding my face and hand. "Shit, I'm so close, baby. Don't you dare fucking stop." I redoubled my efforts, pressing my fingers inside her and sucking hard on her clit.

She cried out, throwing her head back. Her fists tightened around my hair, pulling my face harder onto her crotch. Her breathing became ragged as her pussy pulsed around my fingers. I continued to work them in and out of her, extending her orgasm. When she finally settled, I broke free and rose to my feet.

I scooped her up in my arms and carried her to the bed, a man on a mission.

"Lily, I'm going to fuck you now. I'm going to fuck you hard. I can't wait any longer." I reached for a condom, but she dove for me, fisting my cock in her hand. I froze, my breath hissing out between my teeth as she squeezed me.

She didn't utter a single word. Neither did I.

Her lips closed around me, her tongue stroked along the underside and teased the head. I gave in, falling back against my pillows. I gripped the sheets hard, my fingers threatening to tear the thin material.

Lily hollowed her cheeks, her breathing loud through her nose. Her mouth was hot and wet, the softness of her probing tongue at odds with the intractable hardness of the roof of her mouth.

I hummed low in my throat, letting her hear my approval. Her fist around the base of my dick tightened in response, her head bobbing up and down, wet slurping sounds teasing me. My breath caught.

"Touch my balls," I rasped.

She hummed, the vibrations pulsing through my entire body. She massaged my balls, first one, then the other. Her fingernails gently grazed the sensitive skin, putting me on edge, making me moan.

I wanted to come in her mouth. I wanted to shoot my load down her throat. Needed to feel her squeezing the hell out of my cock as she swallowed every drop I had to give her. Thoughts of it consumed me, but I fought them down.

I'd said I was going to fuck her, and damn it, I was not going to let her take control.

"Enough," I snarled. I grabbed her by the hair and pulled her away. She gasped but released me, allowing me to haul her up to my waiting mouth.

I kissed her, sucking her lower lip into my mouth and biting it, then finally rolled on that condom.

I climbed on top of her, gripped my cock, and lined myself up with her soaking wet pussy. She was so turned on, so hot for me, her entire body screaming for mine. She bit down hard on my shoulder as I thrust into her. Lily's snug pussy enveloped my cock in wet warmth. Her insides caressed my length, squeezing me tight. I swiveled my hips and drove myself even harder. She writhed beneath me, loving every moment and spurring me on further.

I lifted her legs and placed them over my shoulders, rearing up over her. This position was so much deeper as she took me all the way to the hilt, crying out with every thrust. I pounded into her, harder and faster. My balls slapped rhythmically against her ass. Before I knew it, I felt the telltale signs of the beginnings of my impending orgasm, but I wasn't ready to stop yet. I lowered her legs and pulled out, kissing her gently.

Lily cupped my face, confusion in those dark eyes. "Why are we stopping?"

"No questions right now. *Shh* … I want to see you ride me." Without waiting for her to answer, I rolled over onto my back. Lily was quick to climb on top of me, straddling my waist and letting me feel her wetness on my stomach.

"Fuck me, Lily. I want to see you pleasure yourself. Show me how you move, what makes you scream."

Lily reached behind her and gripped my dick to hold where she wanted it, and eased down onto me. She rose all the way up my length a few times, letting the crown almost reach her entrance, then lowered down. Her hands pressed down on the bed just above my shoulders, eyes closed and hair framing her face. She looked like a fucking angel.

I reached up and massaged her breasts, my eyes locked on hers. I rolled her nipples between my fingers, pinched them hard. She gasped and cried out as she arched her back, pulling away from my greedy hands.

Lily leaned forward and kissed me, her rhythm changing along with her position. No longer did she lift up and down. Rather, Lily ground her hips back and forth, my cock buried deep inside. As bashful and awkward as she'd seemed when we first met, not a trace of that could be seen now. She was an erotic seductress, pleasuring herself as I'd demanded.

"Oh fuck, Lily, you're so—" She silenced me with a brief kiss, then again went back to rocking back and forth. She threw her head back and groaned, a primal sound of erotic bliss.

"I'm almost there," she cried out. Her words were enough to push me over the edge. My balls tingled. Pleasure radiated from the base of my spine, making my nipples hard. I knew my own release was imminent.

"Come for me, Lily!" I slapped her ass, and she cried out again as her body pulsed around me, which set off my own climax. My load built up in my balls, the pressure forcing it powerfully upward through my stiff rod. We stayed there for a long time, my dick still inside her, and exchanged gentle kisses. She squeezed me occasionally with her pussy, enjoying the way I gasped each time.

"Stay with me tonight?"

She smiled and slid off me, curling up at my side. "I thought you'd never ask."

I kissed her on the top of the head. "Goodnight, baby."

"Xander?"

"Hmm?"

"Have you ever been in love?"

I stood and walked to the light switch and shut it off before rejoining her. "I thought I was, once. When I was very young."

"What happened?"

"The same thing that inevitably happens with relationships like that. We were kids. It was puppy love. Nothing more."

"That's it, then?"

"Nothing more to tell."

"I'm so sorry."

"Don't worry about me. I turned out just fine. Love is the opiate of the masses, and I decided to be drug-free."

"I guess you're right. Just seems odd to me. Doesn't seem natural to *choose* to be alone."

I sighed. This conversation was headed in a direction I'd rather avoid. No more pillow-talk. No more questions. "Goodnight, Lily."

CHAPTER TEN

I woke from a dream of auburn curls and green eyes to an empty bed. I sat up and stretched. Those damned dreams continued to plague me and I didn't know why. Faith Richardson, that reporter from so many months ago. She had seemed lost, vulnerable. I had agreed to that damned interview here in my home and she had disarmed me at every turn. There had never been anything between us, but ever since that encounter, she had been a specter haunting my subconscious.

I needed to purge her from my system. Faith was my past. Lily was my now. I'd seen no sign of Faith since the interview, and dreaming of someone I'd never had or have was unacceptable.

Where had Lily gone, anyway?

After answering nature's call, I surveyed the bedroom. The bed was a mess. The cards were still strewn across the table. I put on a pair of jeans, then sat on the chair and rewrapped my right ankle before I headed down.

All was dark downstairs; no sign of Lily's presence in the kitchen or living room. I checked the guest room, but I would have been shocked to find her in there; I still hadn't cleaned up from the day before. I unhooked each of the four corners of the fitted sheet and mattress pad, then gathered all the bedding together and dumped them in a corner. I'd just throw that set away, it would be easier than cleaning. I could always pick up more.

Where the hell had Lily gone? I didn't think she'd just leave without saying goodbye. I doubted she'd been paying enough attention to give directions or the address to a friend or a cab company.

She had to be in my gym. Only place she could be that I hadn't checked. I didn't like that she was just making herself at home in there.

My suspicions had been correct. Through the slightly cracked-open doors I saw Lily. Quietly, I pulled the door open and watched her. I wanted to be angry, but my breath caught at the sight of her. My initial displeasure at her being in my personal space without me withered when I caught sight of her. Especially when I pictured what we did the last time we were here together. Now, though, she stood all the way on the other side of the room, reading a framed sheet of paper on the wall.

I knew what it was, too. I wished she hadn't seen it, though she may have already known. It wouldn't have surprised me to know she'd read the article Faith had written about me.

What I want to be when I grow up.

When I grow up, I want to be an Olympic gymnast. I want to compete and I want people to watch me on television and be proud of me. I love birds. Birds can fly and I wish I could, too. Being a gymnast is the closest thing to flying. I bet gymnasts really feel alive.

Emblazoned on the top of the paper was a huge red letter F. It was circled, and in hard block lettering underneath were the words, *Gymnasts can't fly and this dream is virtually unachievable. Be a pilot.*

Great. I should really take that thing down if I'm gonna keep letting people in here.

I stepped inside and approached her. I had kept that paper to remind me of how I had felt that day as a child. I had been homeschooled by my mother, but my father had taken over grading my work because she had been sick. His words had inspired me to prove him wrong, and now look at me. I'd won three gold medals and a silver in last year's Olympics. At the Games before that, I'd won two gold and three silver medals. I'd taken home countless prizes and awards from all over the world, and I was all but a shoo-in for the next

Olympics. I just needed to keep my eyes on the prize. I'd been far too complacent these past few days. Thinking of that paper reminded me of my goals; guess I'd have to keep it after all.

Lily turned away from the wall, raising her cell phone to text someone or take a picture, I wasn't sure which. I paused to watch, but she screeched and dropped her phone.

"Jesus, Xander, you scared the shit out of me!" She whirled around and scooped up her phone, glaring at me.

"What are you doing here?" I prowled toward her, my beautiful prey. She had put on her tiny little skirt and tank top from the night before, and I could see *everything* when she'd bent over, her thong hiding nothing.

"Exploring. Trying not to disturb you." She blushed a bright shade of red and glanced guiltily at her phone. Alarm bells rang in my head, but I disregarded them.

"I woke up to an empty bed. I thought you'd left."

"Where would I go? You drove me here, remember?"

"Didn't put that much thought into it." I watched her intently, willing her to tell me what was in her head right now. "Something wrong?"

She shifted her weight and smiled. "No. Everything is fine. Just thinking of all I still have to get done today. Incidentally, do we have a plan for today, Xander?"

I chuckled. "I have no plan. I keep telling you that. Why don't you tell me about all your plans?"

She shrugged. "Just work stuff. And personal stuff."

"What are you going to do about tomorrow?"

Her eyebrows shot up, almost disappearing into her hairline. "What about tomorrow?"

"Are you going to go back to work?"

She looked uncomfortable, nervous. "I don't know. I'm too afraid not to, but too embarrassed to go." She paused. "My choices are limited. I can walk in there, fight the embarrassment, and act like nothing happened and continue with my job, or I can quit. It's a cut-throat business, and I have to stay ahead of the game. I'm not sure I have the stomach for it anymore." She bit her lip. "On the other hand, it's good money if I can get a good story. I just don't know what else I *could* do. I'm so close to a promotion."

"Tell me about this promotion."

"One of our editors is retiring, which will leave an opening. Amara and I are competing for that position. If I can get it, I'll get better pay and I won't have to dig around in people's personal affairs anymore. My least favorite part of the job."

My heart went out to her. "There must be something I can do to help."

She gave me a hopeful expression, then dropped her gaze to the padded floor, staring at it as if she'd never seen it before. She shook her head. "There's nothing. I should be getting home soon, though."

"Why? Spend the day with me."

Get it together, Xander. You don't get attached to women, remember? This weekend has gone far enough already. Maybe she'll let you fuck her once more, then just take her home. You can't get attached. God damn it.

My subconscious was right. If she wanted to go, I should let her. Despite my claims to Lily about wanting to see where things went, this was all really just about sex, right?

The thing about one night stands was that there were never any messy emotions involved. No worrying about asshole exes or defending my conquest from guys with date rape drugs. No hurt feelings or attachments. I'd never allowed myself to get close to anyone. Now that I'd allowed myself to get close enough to *feel,* I had to acknowledge that the sentiments were confusing. I wanted my life back. I wanted her to go… even as I needed her to stay.

"I'd like to, really. To be honest, though, I'm sore from the last couple of days, and if I stay I'll just end up hurt… in every sense of the word."

This interested me. I made her sore… deep down, I liked that. Meant that she could feel me every time she moved. But…

"I'd never hurt you, Lily." I wouldn't. Not on purpose. "In every sense of the word," she'd said. What kind of monster did she think I was?

Guilt welled up in my chest, followed by a strange sensation. Was it regret? No… that wasn't it. I just didn't want her to leave. I wanted her to stay with me.

"We could…" I trailed off, trying and failing to get a grip on my own wayward thoughts. "If you want to go home, I'll take you."

She looked as confused as I felt. She hesitated, obviously undecided. I hoped she would ask to stay. "Yes."

Damn it! I fought to resist the sudden and unexpected pain, banishing it to wherever it came from. Whatever. That's fine. She wanted our time together to end; that was on her. I would not be the asshole who forced her to stay. "All right. I'll just go finish getting dressed. Be back down in a minute." My voice was harsher than I intended, but so be it. I gestured for her to precede me out of the room. She sat on the couch and buried her head in her hands. I climbed the steps to find a shirt.

CHAPTER ELEVEN

I awoke the next morning with a crazy, half-formed plan in my head. On the drive to Lily's place the day before, she had talked some more about how embarrassed she was that her ex had been cheating on her with her coworker and she'd been none the wiser. When we arrived, I had walked her to her door and kissed her goodbye. I had never meant for there to be anything between us. The rational part of my brain told me to forget I'd ever met her, but the rest of me demanded I see her again, and soon.

I had gone home and spent the rest of the day, well into the evening, working out and going through my routines. Sam had come over to spot me and offer his insights... and well-intentioned harassment. Sam had grilled me about Lily, displeased at my level of distraction, and had relentlessly questioned me while I was trying to stop myself from dwelling on her. Finally, physically and mentally exhausted, I had eaten dinner and gone to bed.

I could show up at *Celebrities and Sinners* and surprise her with flowers. Make a real production of it, help her show her ex what he'd lost. But was that really a good idea? I mean, I didn't really want him realizing what he had done. What if he changed his mind and she took him back? What if she didn't ever want to see me again, anyway? But... what if this *was* what she needed? I could save her pride and maybe keep her from quitting. Perhaps she'd appreciate the effort.

Who was I kidding? I really just wanted to see her again. Fuck this. What had gotten into me? I didn't chase women, they chased me. I stopped and stared at myself in the mirror. When the hell had I shaved and gotten dressed to go? I'd even rewrapped my ankle. I scowled and spoke to my reflection. "You, my friend, are one fucked-up, confused asshole."

Forty-five minutes later, I pulled into the parking lot outside of *Celebrities and Sinners,* two dozen colorful roses artfully arranged in a vase on the floor of the passenger side. I still hadn't made up my mind over whether this was really a good idea or not, but I was here.

What was the worst that could happen?

She could get pissed and never want to see me again, I supposed, but isn't that where our strange relationship was heading anyway? She'd never go for my rigorous "work" schedule. It's easy to get caught up in the excitement but get bored when one sees how much time and preparation goes into professional gymnastics. Besides, that would always be my first love. She'd never settle, and why should she? That didn't mean I couldn't do some good for her here.

I walked through the front doors as if I owned the place. A quick glance at the directory on the wall told me that her office was on the third floor, so I hit the call button for the nearby elevator. A blonde woman stepped in after me, and the doors closed behind her. She made no move to hit the button for another floor. I could feel her eyes locked on me as the elevator lifted skyward.

"I'm curious what horrible crime you committed." Her voice was raspy and throaty, almost a purr, probably from smoking.

"What?"

"The flowers," she elaborated with a chuckle. "Must have been a doozy to warrant so many."

"Not this time." I smiled politely. The elevator chimed, and the doors slid open. I held out my arm to prevent them from closing as she passed.

The entry to *CaS* resembled the waiting room of a doctor's office. Sterile, clinical. Not what you'd expect from a rag. I'd imagined there would be blown-up pictures and articles all over the walls, but they were barren and dull. Blondie headed toward a door to the right, while I approached the open sliding glass window. A woman with ebony skin and tight braids smiled at me from behind her desk.

"I'm here to see Ms. Lily Campbell."

Blondie jerked to a stop halfway through the door and stopped to gawk at me. When she noticed my annoyed glare, she quickly turned away and continued through the door.

"I'll let her know you're here, Mister…?"

"Phoenix. Alexander Phoenix."

Her eyebrows shot up. "Of course, Mr. Phoenix." She picked up a phone and closed the glass window. A few moments later the door swung open, and Lily stood gawking at me from the other side.

"What are you doing here?"

"I came to see you, of course. What else would I be doing here? And look, I brought you flowers."

She dropped her gaze to look at them and pursed her red lips. An unnamed emotion passed over her face. Was she annoyed? Was she trying not to smile? I wasn't sure.

"Why?"

"Because I wanted to, Lily. Because I can. Are you going to show me around or just continue glaring at me?" She glanced back through the door, and I took her moment of indecision as an opportunity to close the distance between us. Three long strides brought me to within a few inches of her, and I reached out to tip her chin back toward me. "Come on, Lily," I murmured, "let me in."

Lily's eyes darkened and her breath came fast. I had her right where I wanted her. No matter what she tried to say now, her subconscious reactions screamed her desire to me. Giving in, she slowly stepped aside to allow me to pass. I took her hand and squeezed it. Looking around, I realized I'd stepped into a strange realm of cubicles. A nine-to-fiver's hell. Real offices lined the walls, but small spaces separated only by low, glass walls filled the center.

"There's really not much to see here," Lily said. "The editors, photographers, and other VIPs are in the outer offices. The journalists are in the center. Through those doors on the other side are break rooms, storage closets, and copy rooms."

I hesitated. Something about her tone sounded off. She spoke to me the way a stranger would, not like someone being visited at work by their prospective boyfriend. "Show me your desk."

Lily tried to pull away, but I tightened my grip on her hand. After a moment, she gave in and led me to her desk. I set the vase in the center of her workspace and smiled down at her, skimming my thumb over her knuckles. "Do you like them?"

She stared at them like she was just seeing them for the first time. "They're beautiful, Xander, but what are you really doing here?"

I traced her lower lip with my thumb and smiled. "I missed you."

Oh, shit. I actually did miss her, I think. I know I said that to her during poker, but... shit. I think it might be true. What the hell is wrong with me?

She smiled, and I pulled her into my arms, ignoring the curious stares from her coworkers. Without moving, I searched the room for someone that could be Michael, her ex. Blondie stared at me from a few desks away, looking like someone had stolen her cigarettes. Briefly, I wondered if this was the infamous Allison.

Lily stiffened and pulled away.

"What?"

"You're embarrassing me," she hissed. "Look around. Everyone is watching us. Why are you here?"

Not the reaction I'd expected. Well, I suppose I'd always known it was a possibility, but I'd hoped she would have been happy to see me. I'd come so everyone would stare. How could she not realize that? Or that I'd done it for her?

"I—"

"Xander, this is a tabloid. You couldn't have nosier people all gathered in one place. Why are you *here*?" she demanded, her voice a cold whisper.

Time to explain. "I'm here to help y–"

"Oh my God, Xander, you're here!" Amara shrieked as she bounded over like a puppy—an annoying puppy. "It's so awesome you've agreed to let her write your story."

"Story?" I frowned at Amara, who stood in front of us gripping a folder, then at Lily. Amara's expression was one of happy curiosity. Lily looked mortified. "What story?"

"The story about the two of you, of course. Of this weekend. What story did you think I meant?"

"Xander…" Lily's voice was strained, her eyes pleading with me. She shook her head almost imperceptibly. Fuck this shit. Lily had guilt written all over her face. I should have known. The signs had been there, but I hadn't wanted to see them. Damn her.

Amara handed me the folder, and an old newspaper article fell out. There were two pictures on it. The first was my sister's smiling face, a picture she'd had taken her senior year in preparation of high school graduation. She was smiling, healthy, beautiful. That picture was the closest she'd get to graduation; she'd died before the semester ended. The other, an ambulance on a beach. I recognized it instantly, and my heart plummeted. With a shaking hand, I bent to pick up the paper and crumpled it into a ball.

"Enjoy your flowers, Lily." Without another word, I stomped from the room and down the stairs, unwilling to wait for the elevator.

She'd played me.

Fuck her. Sam was right. What's worse, it pissed me off that I was running away like a pussy, but I really had no choice. I had been surrounded by tabloid reporters. Anything I said or didn't say would be used against me.

How the hell had she put all that together so quickly? We'd only met last Friday, and it was still early Monday morning. None of this made any sense. I paused. Why would that shit even be relevant in a story about *me*, unless—

No. She couldn't have found out. Those records were sealed. As far as anyone knew, she'd just been a kid who'd made a careless mistake.

"Xander?" Lily called after me as I made it outside. I paused, the rage inside me barely contained as I slowly turned to face her.

"What the hell do you want now? I don't give interviews to women I've fucked."

Lily blanched. "I deserved that," she whispered.

I stared at her impassively. "That's all I needed to know."

"No, it really isn't. Xander–"

"Save it, Lily. You used me."

"Xander, I wasn't going to write the story."

"Why don't I believe you? My family is off limits. Period. Why do reporters always have to poke around people's families? What is the matter with you? And… were you taking pictures in my home gym yesterday?"

She flushed crimson. She was guilty. Why had I dismissed what I'd seen so easily? "Why did you come here today?"

"You've got balls to be questioning me, Lily."

She folded her arms, fire flickering in her eyes. Damn, she was hot when angry. Too bad she was also a manipulative bitch. This was a waste of time.

I'd give her one chance to resolve this. But it would be in the privacy of my house. *Not* in full view of countless tabloid employees.

With a snarl of frustration, I grabbed her hand and pulled her over to my car, flinging open the passenger door. "Get in the car, Lily."

"I have to get back to work."

"Then why the fuck did you come down here?"

She stared at me, defiant. I could hear the blood pounding in my head. This was it. She could come with me and we could sort this shit, or she could choose the job she wasn't sure she wanted in the first place. Was it unfair of me? Absolutely, but at that moment I didn't give a shit.

She slowly approached me and lifted her hand, cupping my cheek. I glared at her, furious, my fists clenched at my sides. She stroked my face, her fingers skimmed over the outer shell of my ear. I leaned my face into her hand and exhaled heavily. "Get in the damn car, Lily."

"Listen, I wasn't going to write the story. I mean... I *was* going to write it, back before we'd met. I swear, Xander, I didn't know you when I started down this path. And then we met and you were so... I don't know. Hot. Mysterious. The sex was incredible, for sure. And there was all that stuff with the guy from the club, and you helped me. I know we didn't really do anything other than have sex together, but you sort of got under my skin. I care about what you think. I didn't have the heart to go public with what I'd found. But I was stuck, Amara was going to write an article about the guy you punched Saturday night, and I told her I was already covering that in *my story*. I was trying to protect you from her."

I said nothing, just stared into her brown eyes.

"I'm not going to lie. This article could help my career... Your past is, well, exciting. Now it has our personal spin on it, and how often does the reporter get an inside scoop like this? But…" She bit her lip. "I couldn't do that to you, to us."

"Lily. Car. Now." I pointed.

"No, Xander. I have to go back to work. Can we talk later?"

What?

Something she had just said stuck out to me. What did she mean, she didn't know me when she started writing the article? "When we met in the club, you didn't recognize me."

"I *did* recognize you," she whispered. "I'd been… researching your story the entire week before. I couldn't believe my good luck when you walked in, when you approached me. I'd never been so flattered in my entire life. You actually noticed *me*."

I stared at her in silence, my blood boiling. She had played dumb. She knew who I was all along. She really had played me.

"Please, Xander, tell me why you came here. I know it wasn't to bring me flowers. You could have gotten those delivered if that's all it was."

I sighed. "Not that it matters now, but I was trying to help you."

"Help me? How?"

"I wanted you to be able to show those assholes that you didn't need them. That you had…"

150

Her face lit up. "Xander Phoenix! You came to help me make my ex jealous?"

I cleared my throat. "Not exactly. Something like that, I guess. I just didn't want you feeling sad and embarrassed. Now, will you *please* get in the car?"

"No. I'm supposed to be working."

"They think you're writing an exposé on us. Call up there and tell them you're working on your article."

"That could work, except I'm not really writing one. They'll notice."

I fought the urge to roll my eyes. I knew I shouldn't try to force her to leave. It was the middle of the work day. Despite that, she had fucked up. She had delved into my personal life on false pretenses and, most damning, had never even told me. She had lied to me.

Would I have been okay with it had she been upfront? Maybe. I had done interviews before. Had she left my family out of it, she would have had a better shot. Besides, she was just a reporter for some irrelevant rag. Her article would probably appear alongside one claiming Michael Phelps was from Mars, had green skin, and wore a human suit to blend in.

I grabbed her and pulled her close, kissing her, forcing my tongue into her mouth. I poured all my feelings of fury, passion, and confusion into that kiss, trying to put everything on display. This was it. If she wouldn't come with me, we were done. No compromise. I released her and backed away, trying to catch my breath. I waited in silence for her decision.

We stared at each other like a couple of fools. What was she thinking? Fuck this. Time was up. Pay or play time. I opened my mouth, but she cut me off with a wave of her hand. She drew herself up to her full height.

"Goodbye, Xander. Thanks for everything. I had a great time this weekend." She held out her hand for me to shake.

What? She was the one who had fucked up, yet she was giving me the brush-off? And offering me nothing but a handshake. Rage coursed through my body, and it was all I could do to maintain my outward calm.

"Lily. The pleasure was mine." Ignoring her hand, I got into the car. I glanced back at her as I punched the bright red button for the ignition, but she was already walking back into her building.

Goodbye, Lily. Pain lanced through my heart, replacing the fury. None of that was how I'd expected this to go.

CHAPTER TWELVE

"No, no, no! What the hell is the matter with you, Phoenix?" Sam's voice echoed in the expanse of my gym. It had been four long weeks. I tried to throw myself into my gymnastics, preparing for a major qualifying event coming up next week right here in Orlando, but my heart wasn't in it… and Sam knew it.

"Sorry, Sam." My voice was lackluster, strained. Sam ran his hands through his hair.

"Where did your focus go? Tell me you aren't still mooning over that girl. It's been a *month!* Let it fucking go already. Your positioning is sloppy. Your landings are terrible. You're not even going to be a contender for the next Olympics if you don't snap out of this shit."

He was right and I knew it. Gymnastics was my first love… but all I could focus on were soft curves and crimson lips. They haunted my memory. The image of Lily, her hand held out for me to shake in farewell.

The ultimate cold shoulder.

She'd invaded my dreams as well, as recently as last night. It started out the same as always: the reporter with auburn hair and green eyes. She stood naked before me, unashamed and stunning. As I reached for her, though, her irises darkened to brown. Her body and face thinned out and her hair lightened to dirty blonde. Lily glared up at me, then turned and walked away. I had dreamed of her walking away from me countless times since that horrible Monday. I was bone-tired. Was it any wonder I couldn't focus?

"Alexander!"

Shit. I realized Sam had been talking this whole time. My mind had wandered. *"What?"* I snapped.

"What the fuck is your problem?"

I shrugged.

"You've been a mess since your drug scare. You've lost your edge, man. What the hell am I here for?"

"I'm fine."

"You're *not* fine."

"Leave it, Sam."

"Tell me what the hell your problem is and I'll consider it."

"I said fucking leave it," I snarled.

"There we go. There is some of the fire we've been lacking. It's *her*, isn't it? That woman that got drugged. She messed you up big time."

"Leave her out of this."

"What I don't understand is how she got under your skin. What was so special about her? You've been with countless others and never thought twice about them."

A fair question. The fight went out of me, and I slumped onto the mat. "She was the first one I sort of cared about, and she was the first to tell me no. To turn her back on me."

"Dude, you sound like a chick. Snap out of it and get your shit together. Now."

"Don't you think I want to?"

"Let's call it for tonight. God knows we're not doing any good here. Relax and get your act together. *Then*, we'll try this again. Also, *no* booze. No women. I'm not kidding. You're screwed up enough and you have a qualifier."

I nodded. Sam grabbed his stuff and left me in the silence of my house. I contemplated what to do. Sam said no booze or women, but already I was considering how *both* of those things might improve my general outlook. It was Saturday, but too early to hit a club. I needed to clear my head. I could go for a run, but the Orlando humidity was stifling. I picked up my cell and checked my weather app. Not too bad. I'd try it. I laced up my running shoes and headed out.

My feet pounded the pavement, and I let my mind wander as I hit my stride. This was a great idea, no focus required. I just had to pay enough attention to not get hit by a car. After that dismal practice session, my thoughts inevitably turned to Lily.

That bitch had tricked me into giving a shit about her when she had been playing me the entire time. Despite all that, I still had some insane desire to clear the air between us. I'd nearly called her so many times, but my own stubbornness had stopped me. I knew I didn't like feeling like this. I didn't love her, but I definitely felt something for her. Was it just lust? The only way to find out would be to try to continue our relationship. Only problem was I couldn't control her. It drove me insane. I had tried; I told her to get in the car and she'd refused.

Had she just been jerking me around for her article? I hadn't seen one, but I hadn't really looked, either. No one paid any attention to tabloid articles, so why should I care? Furthermore, what was with me and reporters lately? Newspaper reporters, tabloid reporters… they were all bad news. I should steer clear.

I neared a bar and grill with outdoor seating, and I slowed to a stop.

A balding man with wire-rimmed glasses and a bad comb-over sat with a young woman. They both looked so familiar. I doubled over to catch my breath, sneakily looking closer.

Holy shit. Mr. Retirement Fund… and Amara.

Did she know who he was, or was this a chance encounter? Did he know she was a tabloid reporter? Was she setting him up? Was he planning to attack her? I turned my back, dropping down to tie my shoes, trying to listen in.

"… it wouldn't be so hard to get to her if you hadn't screwed it up in the first place," Amara hissed, her tone accusatory. They were a fair distance away, and the street noises made it difficult to hear them. I strained my ears, still crouched on the ground, all pretext of tying my shoes gone. "I paid you good money to take Lily away and get those pictures of her. Now how am I going to guarantee I get the promotion?" That last word was almost an unintelligible shriek.

I couldn't believe it. It sounded like Lily getting drugged wasn't a random incident; it had been orchestrated by her friend. Over a job. I was shocked that anyone could stoop that low. I straightened up to my full height and opened the gate separating the covered seating area from the passersby.

"Amara." I bit out her name and nodded to her, my arms crossed. "Who's your friend?"

"Xander!" she gushed. "Isn't this a pleasant surprise? This is my business associate, Carl Franco. Carl, Xander Phoenix. Please, won't you join us?"

"This isn't a social visit. I heard what you two were talking about."

Amara's face contorted in rage, while Franco's already pale complexion lightened further. "And what do you *think* you heard, exactly?"

My hands clenched into fists. I had to keep my cool. She would not provoke me. She didn't want to dance with me, not here, not in public. I raised my voice. "I heard you say that you paid this m–"

"Keep your voice down!" Franco jumped to his feet and lunged around the table as though he were going to run. I was faster. His shirt clenched tight in my fist, I jerked him toward me and punched him. Pain, sharp and hot, raced through my hand as I felt his nose give way, submitting to the force of my blow. His body went slack. He fell hard to the ground, knocking a metal chair aside.

The noise of the other guests died away, leaving a bubble of silence only broken by the road noise nearby. Amara pulled out her smartphone, the screen flashing to life. I held out a hand to stop her.

"Don't even think about it. Either of you. Just so you know, I have full toxicology reports on both Lily and myself. We have witnesses. I know what you did. You, Franco, are in deep shit. My advice? Get the fuck out of here."

"It's your word against ours, Xander." Amara's voice was pure malice. "Do you think Lily would testify against me?"

"Maybe. Maybe not. I know she would against your friend here." I pointed at Franco with my uninjured hand. Blood gushed from his nose and covered his face, rendering him unrecognizable. "Deep shit, asshole. Remember that."

I stomped out the gate without a backward glance, waving off an indignant looking waitress.

Blood leaked out of small gashes in my sore knuckles. *Shit.* Sam was going to kick my ass when he caught wind of this. I flexed my hand, wincing. I'd gotten off lucky. I didn't think anything was broken except the skin.

I'd worry about my hand soon enough. First, I needed to see Lily. I broke into a jog, my thoughts a jumbled mess as I thought about what I would say to her.

I trotted up the stairs and flung open my bedside table, searching without success for the card she had given me. I knew it had to be in there. Just when I was starting to get really aggravated, I found it.

I quickly programmed the number into my phone. I should have done this long ago; it just never came up. I punched dial and waited. It went to voicemail.

"Um, hi. Lily? It's Xander. Listen, I know we haven't spoken in a while, but I need to talk to you, and it's kind of important. Give me a call at this number when you get my message. Thanks. Bye." I hit disconnect and stared at the phone, half expecting it to ring immediately. Turning the volume way up, I set the phone on the bathroom counter and switched the shower on. I had no idea if she would call me back in five minutes or five hours, or if she would even call me back at all, but I wanted to be ready if and when she did.

I showered quickly, toweling off my hair and body before wrapping the towel around my waist. Fishing out a bandage, I wrapped my hand, then grabbed my laptop off the bedside table.

Pulling it up, I used their search box to find articles Amara had written. Thank God her name hadn't been Susan or Cathy or something common. Pausing over the large listing of articles, I highlighted her name. Amara Dagher. I opened another window and typed her name into the search bar. Dozens of pictures of her came up. Professional pictures, candid pictures, old MySpace pictures. I scrolled through them all, searching for any that might have Mr. Retirement Fund in them. Clicking on a Facebook photo, I opened up her personal page.

Like mine, her page was wide open so the whole world could see it. Not sure why she hadn't tightened it down or made it friend only, but so much the better for me. I quickly flipped through her pictures and started reading her status updates.

The phone rang, startling me from my concentration. I jumped and knocked the phone onto the floor. I bent to pick it up with a shaking hand, my heart pounding from the shock.

Lily.

My mouth went dry.

What the fuck is the matter with me?

"Phoenix."

"Xander, it's Lily. I was returning your call?" She sounded hesitant; her voice was breathy and brought to mind the way she sounded when I was inside her. *Focus, Xander.*

"Lily, yes. I found out something about..." Shit, what was I going to say? How could I bring this up? "About... Lily, can I see you?"

Silence was my answer. Finally, "I'm not sure that's such a good idea."

"Lily, I need to talk to you. It's important, and this is really hard to discuss over the phone. Please?"

Lily paused. "All right. Meet me in the IHOP you took me to. Do you remember which one?"

"Yes. When?"

"An hour?"

"I'll be there. See you soon."

I ended the call and returned to my search.

CHAPTER THIRTEEN

My search hadn't pulled up ay relevant information. The name Carl Franco had brought up hundreds of names, and cross-referencing with Amara's profile had been another dead end. She wasn't friends online with anyone by that name. Whatever. Had I found actual proof that they knew each other, it would have been great, but I wanted Lily to believe me over her lying bitch of a friend, even without proof.

Perhaps I should have brought flowers. Oh well, too late now. I entered the diner and requested a table by the front window. I ordered each of us a glass of water with lemon and settled down to wait.

Every time a car approached, my pulse sped. Why was I such a nervous wreck? Sure, I had information for her that she wouldn't like, but why would that have any effect on me? I took a deep breath and checked the time.

She was fifteen minutes late. I sighed in frustration. She said she would be here, but where was she?

Suddenly, there she was, walking around the building and in front of my window. A frisson of excitement jolted through my veins. Even in the yoga pants and loose-fitting oversized top she wore, she was sexy. Her eyes were bright, and her pink cheeks made her almost look like she was glowing. I realized I was glad to see her. I rose to my feet as she entered and approached my table.

"Xander… you look good."

"So do you. Please, sit down." I held out her chair.

"Sorry I was late."

"No problem. I wasn't waiting long."

"What's going on?"

I hesitated. "How have you been?"

What looked like alarm passed over her lovely face, but it disappeared quickly. "I've been fine. You said you needed to talk to me, that it was important."

"How have things been with you and Amara?"

"You brought me here to discuss Amara?" she demanded, her voice low and dangerous. She tapped her fingernails against the tabletop.

"Has she called you recently?"

"Why? You want to hook up with *her* now? You think I'm your way in?"

"Lily, it's not like that. Hear me out before you get mad, okay? This is important. Yeah, this is about Amara, but it's about you, too."

Lily folded her arms in front of her chest, almost as if she were protecting herself from me. "Fine, go on."

"How long have you known her?"

"Why?"

"Answer me?"

"Why should I?"

I stared at her, my annoyance building. I was trying to have a conversation with her, but she insisted on becoming so defensive. Thinking back, she was always defensive when it came to Amara. Time to shock her. No more pussyfooting around.

"I saw her with the man who drugged you. His name is Carl Franco."

Lily froze. Her mouth opened, but no sound came out.

I nodded. "Yup. That's what I wanted to say. I wanted to ease you into it, but I don't know why you're always so defensive."

"Sh–she was... did you warn her?" Lily snatched up her phone and started tapping the screen. "I have to make sure she's okay. Why wouldn't you stop her?"

Shit! She thinks he was going to drug her. I placed my hand atop hers. "Lily..."

She scowled and jerked her hand away.

"Lily, she hired him to take pictures of you in a compromising position. To blackmail you so she would get the promotion."

"No..."

"No?"

"She wouldn't." Her voice was barely more than a whisper.

"What do you mean she wouldn't? Lily, the woman hit on *me* right in front of you. In fact..." I furrowed my brow, thinking, "In fact, that second night in the club, Chrissy told me that guy had approached her but ran off when those two bozos from outside joined her. I'd assumed he'd chosen her for his next mark, but obviously not."

"How do you know all this?"

"I caught them together while out jogging. I stopped and listened in."

"You were eavesdropping?"

"Yes, and aren't you glad I was?"

"I'm sorry, but all this is just a little hard to believe."

And there it is.

"Well, believe it, baby. After I heard what they'd done, I confronted them and broke his nose." I sighed. "Look, we haven't spoken in a month. I've missed you, I admit it. I don't think *lying* to you would be the best way to win your affections back, do you? I'm telling you the truth; *I* have never lied to *you*. Focus on what's important here, Lily."

All the fight went out of her. She looked so lost and forlorn.

"She isn't your friend," I continued. "She paid some guy to drug you. Over a job. That's insane."

She said nothing, merely sat frozen.

"Lily?" I wanted to be closer to her, wanted to take her in my arms and comfort her, but I didn't. No matter how much I wanted her, we still had more to discuss about *us* before I dared touch her.

"I have nothing left," she whispered.

"What?"

"I have nothing left. Michael, Allison, Amara, you… and if all this is true, I don't have a place to live, either."

"Come again?"

"She's my roommate. The apartment is hers." Lily pinched the bridge of her nose, clearly at a loss. "I can't take this anymore, the backstabbing, the rivalries. It's too much."

Damn it! I hadn't seen this coming. What the hell was I supposed to do? How was I supposed to handle this? I sat back in my chair and rubbed my temples. "What will you do?"

Lily threw her hands up in the air. "What can I do? I have nowhere to go. My parents are separated, moved on. They don't live locally. My dad has a single bedroom apartment. My mom has her new family. They have no room for me. I have no friends I can trust, apparently. All I can do is keep going on and just let her have the promotion. Then maybe this will end and she'll leave me alone. I can look for another job and place to stay in my spare time."

"So you aren't going to confront her? She just gets away with it? You're just going to keep living with her after what she did?"

"I don't enjoy sleeping on the streets, so yes."

I knew what I needed to do, knew how I could help her, but I held back. "Lily… tell me about the article. I have to know."

Confusion marred her beautiful face. "What article?"

"Me."

"There was no article. I scrapped everything." Noticing my frown, she leaned forward and placed her hand in mine, her brown eyes meeting my blue. "Xander, I was writing about you before we ever met. I was determined to expose your big secret. I have a source who claimed she knew your sister. Her version of the months leading up to the accident was fascinating to say the least."

Fuck! She *did* find out. I fought to keep my expression bland, not wanting to lend credence to the story.

"I almost told you about it so many times that weekend," she continued, "but we were having such a great time, and I didn't want to risk it. Then you punched that guy in the club."

I grunted. Not my best moment.

"That was sweet and took me by surprise. No one has ever punched anyone else over me before. That said, Amara saw everything. She knew who that guy was," Lily chuckled. "In fact, she did his friend that night. She could have written God only knows what about what she witnessed, and then that man would have recognized you. Could have sued you. I said I was writing it to throw her off the scent. Her limited article would have been boring compared to the dirt I had on you, and she *knew* it."

"Why would you cancel your article for me? I know we had an awesome weekend and all, but one weekend is hardly life altering." Despite my words, the relief washed over me. Lily wasn't going to blast my life, or my family's, in front of the world to sell her story after all.

She bit her lip. "It was for me."

That settled it.

I couldn't let her stay with that treacherous twat she called a friend. Not now.

"Have you folks decided?" I glanced up at the waitress. Where had *she* been all this time? I had

169

decided, all right. I rose to my feet and held out my hand to Lily.

"That won't be necessary. We're leaving."

"We are?" Lily asked.

"Yes." I tossed a few bucks on the table.

"Where is your car?" I asked as we walked outside.

"I walked here."

"Do you actually *have* a car? I've never seen you with one."

"No."

"I'd have picked you up, Lily. You didn't need to walk." I opened up the passenger door. "Get in the car."

"A 'please' would be nice."

I stared at her in stony silence, but she just crossed her arms and glared right back.

Damn it. "Please get in the God damned car."

She slid gracefully in, and I shut the door behind her. Climbing in the driver side, I hit the button for the ignition. Damn, it was stifling in here. I cranked the air conditioner, even though it blew hot air.

"Where are we going?"

"Back to my place, to plan."

"Plan?"

"Well, you didn't think I'd let you go back to the woman who could have killed you, did you?"

"Xander, I told you. I have nowhere to go."

I ran my thumb along her lower lip. It was so plump and soft. I put the car in reverse and backed out of the parking spot.

"Move in with me."

"Wait, *what?*"

I glanced at her, nearly chuckling at the look of shock and horror on her face.

"You heard me."

"You've gone insane since we last met."

"Hardly. Lily, I've missed you. I haven't even admitted to myself how much. Have you missed me?"

"Well, yes, but–"

"I've thought of you every day. Listen, even if you don't want to have a relationship with me, you can move into my spare room for a while. At least until you have everything worked out. Okay? You can put in your notice and start looking for a job. I'll take care of everything in the meantime."

"I don't think that's such a good idea."

I shifted the car into sixth as I merged onto I-4. "Why not?"

"We barely know each other."

"Clearly, you *barely* knew Amara. I, at least, want what's best for *you.* Now we can do this the easy way or the hard way. Just move in with me."

"What's the hard way?"

"You mean besides the obvious?"

"You're such a child. Just answer the question."

"Well, you can just agree and move in willingly… or I can keep insisting until you can't take it anymore. I can argue with you while we drive, I can continue while you pack your things. I can keep going while we carry your things into my house. One way or another, though, you'll give in. You'll give in because it's the right thing to do, or you'll give in to shut me up. The end result is the same."

"My apartment is the other way."

I grinned and took her hand in mine, bringing it to my lips. "You haven't agreed yet. Besides, I'll need to find some help to get your things out of there as quickly as possible so you don't have to be around Amara for long."

"Oh God. I don't even want to think about that."

"So you'll do it?"

Lily jerked her hand back and folded her arms over her belly, pouting. "Yes, damn it."

"Yes, you'll move in with me?"

"Yes," she answered sullenly.

"You don't have to sound so excited about it."

"Not like you really gave me much choice."

"You're right." I reached for her hand again. "But why should I leave you alone to deal with that bitch when I can so easily help you? We'll put your stuff in the guest bedroom, okay? That way there's no pressure. But, Lily…"

"Yes?"

"I've missed us. That weekend meant something to me, too. I've been off my game since we parted ways. I'd like to at least *try* the relationship thing. What do you say?"

I risked a glance at Lily, only to find her gazing at me with a peculiar expression. Something similar to amusement, but not quite. Triumph, maybe? No. That wasn't right, either.

"Is that a yes?"

"Well, it's not a no, but…"

"But?"

"I'd like to learn if we can be friends first, before we jump back into bed again."

"You didn't like the sex?" I was disappointed, but she was still coming home with me. I'd win her over.

"The sex was incredible. Beyond incredible."

That's better. "But?"

"But you're just so overwhelming, and if we're going to try to be together, I'd like it to be based on more than sex. I'll be living there with you, and we'll have time to get to know each other. Let's not force it."

"Good enough."

We spent the rest of the drive back making idle chit-chat, my heart feeling lighter than it had in weeks.

CHAPTER FOURTEEN

I breezed in from my gym to grab a bottle of water from the fridge. Sam followed behind me, still crowing about how I was going to *own* that event tomorrow evening. He was right; I was ready, focused. I had this in the bag. I grinned at Lily, who stood barefoot in the kitchen, cooking.

The last week had been a blur. I'd called Sam and my buddy John on Sunday morning, and we'd moved her things over in just a couple of hours. Sam wasn't happy. In fact, he was downright pissed about my injured hand. He finally agreed to help after I promised my hand wouldn't be an issue and assured him that I'd be ready and focused at practice.

Amara, of course, had been there. It made for an uncomfortable situation that had worsened by the second. But we'd gotten Lily moved out with minimal arguing and even managed to avoid anyone getting into a fist fight.

Lily was sometimes strangely distant, but I chalked it up to there being so many changes all at once. When I got her to relax, she laughed and smiled. We teased each other and were happy. We had dinner together each night. I wanted her so much, but I respected her wishes to be friends first. Instead, we made out like teenagers and drove each other insane. I had a feeling that whenever she decided we could have sex again, we would end up attacking each other like rabid animals. In the meantime, the unresolved sexual frustration only gave me added energy to work off at practice.

Lily had put in her two weeks' notice at work, but *Celebrities and Sinners* had elected to accept her resignation and cut her loose, naming Amara as their next editor. The plus side was that they gave her a severance package, and it had freed her up to search for a new job. She'd interviewed at local newspapers and hoped to be hired as a real reporter; no more tabloids. At least, that's what she said she wanted. I found that I liked having her here, even if I would rather she was in my bed and not sleeping downstairs.

I checked out Lily's long legs, allowing my eyes to sweep from her toes to her belly. I ogled her ample breasts, the hollow of her throat, and finally up to her lips. "Well, thanks for stopping by, Sam. See you tomorrow morning at the competition."

Sam nodded. "Whatever you're cooking smells great, Lily."

"Sure does. Looks like spaghetti. Shame you have to leave now." I mimed checking a watch on my bare wrist.

Sam laughed and raised his hands in surrender, nodded to Lily, and left.

"Well, that was rude," she scolded.

"Sure was. Not half as rude as what I'd like to do to you."

"I'm cooking. It's almost time to eat."

"I'd like to eat *you*."

She blew on a spoonful of sauce, then licked it off. She closed her eyes and hummed.

"Put the lid on that and move it off the burner," I softly instructed. To my surprise, she complied. Desire consumed me, hot and heady, running through my veins. "Come here."

She walked into my waiting arms. I kissed her, possessing her mouth and tongue with my own. My cock pressed between us, and I had never been so glad to be wearing workout pants. Our breathing became ragged and our tongues twisted in an erotic tango. Her scent surrounded me, overwhelmed me, called to me on a primal level. I yanked her hair back and suckled her neck, moaning my desire.

"Lily… what do you want?"

"You."

Thank God! "I'm glad to hear you say that. I've been waiting for this moment." I lifted her in my arms.

"Put me down, Xander! I can walk."

"Yes, but this is faster, baby." I carried her up the stairs and straight into my room. I set her down and stepped back. "Take off your clothes."

She hesitated and I frowned.

"Now, Lily. Do as I say."

Reluctance and regret passed over her beautiful features, briefly enough to make me question if I'd seen them. She'd looked almost like there was something she wanted to say, but then her face split into a flirtatious grin. "Come and take them off me, Xander."

Tempting. But why can't she ever do as she's told? I prowled toward her, fighting every instinct I had to grab her, rip her clothes off, and make her mine. I wanted her, needed to bury myself in her... but this was still my house, and she needed to remember who was in control.

"Xander?" My name on her lips snapped me back to the here and now. I set my jaw, giving in and pulling her tube top up and over her head. I inhaled sharply as she cupped me through my workout pants.

I lifted her up again and tossed her on the bed. "You need to learn to do as you're told."

"Do I?"

"Yes." I unbuttoned and unzipped her jeans, then gripped them by the waistband and pulled them and her panties down in one fluid motion.

Discarding the clothes in a heap, I loomed over her, supporting my weight on my left arm. I stared straight into her eyes as I slowly inserted two of the fingers of my right hand inside her. "Shit, Lily… you're so wet already."

"Xander, please don't tease me." She bucked her hips up to meet my hand, trying to urge my fingers deeper inside.

"Shh… keep still."

She ground her hips against my fingers again. This would not do. I withdrew and placed my fingers in my mouth. "Mmm… you taste even better than I remember. But you need to do as I say and hold still." I stood up and walked into my closet, grabbing a braided belt. Her breath caught when I emerged and she got a look at it.

"Keep still."

"You aren't going to hit me, are you?"

"Hadn't planned on it. I wouldn't enjoy causing you pain. I do want you to hold still, though." I bound her wrists together. Not tight enough to hurt if she wriggled around—something I had every intention of making her do—but just snug enough to keep her from going anywhere. I didn't really have anywhere to connect it to on this sleigh bed. I lifted her hands and pulled her up so that her fingers brushed the smooth, cool leather of the headboard. "Feel that? Keep your hands there, against the leather. Do not lower them. Do not move at all. Got it?"

She nodded, her brown eyes dark. I watched her for a few moments until I was certain she'd do as she was told.

I leaned over her and brushed my lips across hers, then sucked and licked my way down her chin and neck. Reaching her collarbone, I bit down and sucked the skin into my mouth, reveling in her answering moan. I continued my path; covering every inch of her chest with wet kisses, savoring her. I paused to admire her perfect tits; they looked even bigger and more beautiful than I remembered. Everything was better now. I knew her erect nipples craved my mouth, but I resisted the urge and ran my fingers and teeth down her ribs and toward her navel. She cried out and sucked in her belly, writhing beneath me.

"Keep still," I rasped. To deny myself any longer was a torture I didn't think I could endure. I moved down and to the side, scraping my teeth gently over her hipbone, then kissed and sucked my way over to her other hip and repeated the process. Lily groaned, her hips jerking beneath me.

"Didn't I tell you to keep still? Do you want me to stop?"

"Yes," Lily gasped.

"You want me to stop?"

"Please, Xander, I want you. No more teasing."

"I say when," I snapped. My voice was harsher than I'd intended. I knew I would probably give in, but it would be on my terms, not hers.

"Please, Xander," she begged. "I need your cock inside me now."

Fuck! I wrenched open the drawer in the bedside table and grabbed a condom. Without wasting a moment, I shoved my pants down and rolled it on. Then I was on top of her, the tip of my cock positioned at her slick entrance.

"This is what you want, baby?" *Please say yes.*

"You're what I want, only…"

"Yes?"

"I want to touch you. Please?"

Her desperate plea moved me. I realized I, too, wanted her to touch me.

"Give me your hands." In no time at all, her hands were freed and I'd flung the belt onto the floor. I thrust into her, stilling at the sound of her gasp. "Lily…"

"Hmm?"

"Open your eyes."

Her eyelids fluttered open, and she stared up at me. I lowered myself down and caressed her cheek as I slowly began to move. I saw the emotions I felt reflected back at me in her eyes. It was too much, far too much. I kissed her, my tongue demanding entrance to her mouth. My weight rested on my forearms and, pressing down on her shoulders to hold her in place, we found our rhythm.

I groaned and swiveled my hips, pivoting forward to reach her g-spot.

"Faster, Xander, please." Lily pulled her mouth from mine, panting. She met me thrust for thrust, giving as good as she was taking, encouraging me to drive into her faster, harder. Her nails clawed at my back and begged me to give in.

"Oh, no, baby. This is going to be slow. I want you to feel all of me." I reared up and positioned her legs over my shoulders, only pausing for a moment to reposition.

"Please… fuck me. I want to feel you."

I leaned all my weight on one arm and reached the other down between us to find her clit. I massaged in slow circles, watching her face as the sensations washed over her.

Her cries became more ragged as her impending orgasm drew closer. I wanted to kiss her, to swallow her cries with my mouth, but I wanted to watch her face as she came even more.

Her legs trembled, and I hummed low in my throat. "Come for me, Lily."

Her body shivered as she fell over the precipice. Her pussy squeezed me, milking my cock. I tried to ride it out, didn't want to stop, but her orgasm seemed to go on endlessly. I surrendered to my body. I thrust deep inside and stilled, lost to the sensations as my load spurted, hot and powerful, into her cunt.

"I love you, Xander…"

I froze, positive I had misheard. Her voice had been an almost imperceptible whisper. Without a word, I withdrew and removed the condom, tossing it carelessly toward a trash can. A glance in her direction told me she still watched me expectantly, waiting for me to answer.

"I–what did you say?" I fought back the surge of panic, forcing my expression to remain neutral.

"You didn't hear me, or you wish you didn't hear me?"

Yeah, right. Like I'm dumb enough to fall for that. "The first one. I'm sorry, I thought you said something."

She sat up, regarding me, trying to find the lie on my face. "I said I love you, Xander. I know we haven't known each other long, but this last week has been the best in my entire life."

I opened my mouth, but she cut me off, placing a finger over my lips.

"Shh… there's more. Let me finish. I need to tell you something else. I wasn't sure how you were going to handle it, but you deserve to know."

My heart thudded in my chest as I waited.

CHAPTER FOURTEEN

"I'm pregnant," she whispered.

Chapter Fifteen

"Pregnant?"

The world stopped. My breath rushed out of me like I'd been sucker-punched. I must have misheard her. I jumped to my feet and yanked my pants up, desperate to put some distance between us while I processed this.

"P–pregnant? How?" The surprise that she'd professed her love only a moment before paled and faded, giving way to the much *more* shocking news she'd just delivered. If her goal had been to give me a heart attack, she might still succeed.

She rolled her eyes. "You ask me that not even a minute after pulling your dick out of me?"

"Is it mine?"

"Of course it's yours! Who else's would it be?" She crossed her arms over her chest. "What the hell kind of question was *that*?"

"It could be your ex's. Didn't you break up the same day we met? Did you see anyone after me? I think that's a fair God damned question."

"Michael and I broke up the same day, but we hadn't had sex together for a couple of weeks. I've had my period since then. There's been no one else."

"B–but…" My gaze fell on the used condom on the floor, "but we used protection. Every time. Didn't we?" I thought back to every erotic encounter we had shared those two blissful days. This was a nightmare. Instead of basking in an afterglow with her, I'd had a pretty effective bucket of freezing cold water dumped over me.

"I thought so, too. Looking back, though, there was that time in your gym…"

God damn it. She was right. I remembered it clearly now that she brought it up: the arguing, the banter that led to me falling. I remembered it all, every moment of that tryst playing back through my mind. I hadn't even had pockets. There was no way I'd had a condom. How could I have been so stupid?

"I'm sorry, Xander," she whispered.

I couldn't breathe. The walls closed in on me. I looked down at Lily, every muscle tense, disgust driving my emotions. Disgust at myself… and at her. "How long, Lily?"

"What?"

"How long have you been keeping this from me?"

She flushed. "Three weeks."

Three fucking weeks. Between moving in with me and that first weekend, we'd only spent nine days together. She'd known longer than that. I had to get out of here. I had to leave before I said something I'd *really* regret. I was so furious, yet somehow knew that wouldn't help matters. Something in my brain switched off, checking out. The feelings numbed, the fury abated. I knew they were still there, but my mind repressed them.

"Xander, I–"

I walked back to her and pulled her to her feet. I kissed her, lightly brushing my lips over hers. She didn't react. She didn't melt into me as she had before. I felt... nothing. I released her.

"It'll be okay, Lily. I promise. I... I need to go. I have to think. I'll see you soon, okay?"

"You're leaving?" She looked horrified.

I swallowed. "I have to... for now. I need to get out of here, I need air. Just... I gotta go."

She didn't move, didn't react as I turned my back on her and headed for the stairs and out of my own home.

CHAPTER SIXTEEN

"Next up on rings is Alexander Phoenix, USA."

I lifted my right arm into the air and paused, then ambled over to the rings, waiting. I covered my hands with chalk and adjusted my ring grips. Sam was ready and waiting. At a nod of my head, he placed his hands on my waist and helped me up. I strengthened my grip, calmed my nerves. Blocked out the judges, the crowds, everything. This was my event. I was ready.

I extended my arms to either side and held the Iron Cross, every muscle in my body taut. I curled my legs up into a sitting position and rolled over in a slow somersault. Circling around again, I lifted into a handstand, then swung myself around.

The memory came unbidden to my mind.

"I'm pregnant, Xander."

No.

Not now. I hadn't slept at all last night. I had walked to my buddy John's house and crashed on his couch. I tossed and turned and thought about all my mistakes. Maybe it was her fault; she had been a tabloid reporter. Had she planned to ensnare me? I knew that was wrong, though. She was guilty, yes, but I was just as guilty.

I completed the second circuit around and spread my arms to drop back into the Iron Cross position, but my right hand slipped.

Fuck.

I only had a split second to process what was happening as I crashed to the floor. I tried to catch myself with my left hand, but felt a tearing pain in my shoulder, followed by a worse pain in my back as I landed flat on my tailbone, sitting up.

I was dazed. I'd never fallen like that before. My entire body had tensed as I fell. I tried to get up, but the pain overwhelmed me. I collapsed onto my side and rolled flat onto my back. My stomach roiled, my vision darkened as my breakfast threatened to be forced up and out. Vaguely, almost as if it were happening to someone else, I became aware of the horrified tone of the announcer's voice, the fact that the crowd had gone silent, and worst of all… Sam's terrified face as he tried to get my attention.

"Sam…?"

"Don't move, Xander. The paramedics will have the stretcher here in just a moment."

That's it. He didn't ask me to do anything, didn't ask inane questions about how many fingers he was holding up. He didn't touch me at all, just stood close by, waiting. Clearly, I was too fucked up for there to be any need.

CHAPTER SIXTEEN

What the hell had I done?

CHAPTER SEVENTEEN

I woke to a shrill beep. My eyes jerked open. I tried to focus on my surroundings. I was in a strange bed in a strange white room. The sound came from a slender metal stand next to my bed. A clear, almost empty bag hung from the pole, swinging slightly.

An IV. This was a hospital room. I tried to sit up, but pain ripped through my back and arm, threatening to make me black out. I fumbled for the call button my foggy brain knew had to be there.

The EMTs had determined that I needed X-rays, so they'd brought me to the hospital. My left arm had been dislocated at the shoulder socket. My jaw clenched. Resetting that had been a blast. But the real problem was my back. Worry pooled in my gut. What would become of me?

After the X-rays, they had stuck me in a room and told me that my regular doctor would visit me in the morning. The overnight doc had ordered pain medications, and they'd essentially knocked me out for the night.

My right hand gripped the wired remote that held the call button.

The static-filled voice through the remote sounded tinny, disjointed. *"Your light is on. How can I help you?"*

I cleared my throat. "The IV alarm is going off."

"I'll send in your nurse." The static vanished and, with it, my connection to the outside world. I dropped the remote, exhausted.

What the hell had happened out there? That was my event. *Mine.* All I had had to do was claim it, but I'd lost my focus.

I sighed. I'd lost my focus because my subconscious knew what was really important. *Lily.* She was carrying my child. *My* child. We hadn't known each other long. She'd said this last week was the best in her life. Well, it was one of mine, too. And I'd panicked and walked out on her.

I could never ask Lily to have an abortion. The thought was horrific to me. I was sure she didn't want to, either. If she *had* wanted to end it, wouldn't she have done it already? We'd have to find a way to make this work. We could split time between us like other unmarried parents.

Or, what if Lily could be my future? She *said* she loved me. Did she mean it?

I *could* always propose. That would be the honorable thing to do.

An image formed in my mind: coming home to my family, kissing my wife, having meals together. It looked… right. Things may not be easy as we got to know each other, but we'd find a way.

Feelings of both hope and dread fought for control of my body. Was it wrong of me to think of proposing now that my gymnastics career was almost certainly over? Was I merely facing some sort of existential crisis from the probable loss of my ability to compete anymore? Did this mean I was dumping all my hopes and goals on her? Hell, yeah… and I knew it.

None of that changed the fact that it was still the right thing to do.

I had to get myself together for the sake of our child. I *could* learn to love Lily.

The door swung open, followed by a brief tap. "Can I come in?" I turned to stare, half expecting Lily to walk in, but it was just a blonde woman dressed in bright blue scrubs, dragging a rolling kiosk with a laptop on it behind her.

"You ask me after opening the door? Not like I could stop you even if I wanted to. Come on in. Your hospital."

She smiled and flipped a switch on the IV pole, silencing it. The ringing echoed in my ears in the sudden quiet.

"My name is Corrine, and I am your nurse today. How are you feeling, Mr. Phoenix?"

"Well, as long as I don't move too much, just fine."

"What is your pain level on a scale of one to ten?"

"Sitting still or moving?"

"You tell me."

"Umm... not moving, maybe a four. When I try to sit up..." I tried, gasping at the pain. "Eight."

She tapped away at some keys on the laptop. "It's been about six hours since your last dose of pain medication. I'll bring you more Dilaudid. And more fluids for your IV. Do you need anything else?"

Lily. "No, thank you."

She turned and dragged the rolling kiosk out with her.

I returned to planning out my next moves with Lily. My decision was made, not that I had much alternative. Every other option seemed bleaker than the last. Child support payments? Living alone, bitter, consumed by broken dreams? No, I had to take steps to improve things. We already lived together. After I got discharged I would get a ring and propose. I'd get flowers, play soft music, the works. She'd love it... I hoped.

My gymnastics future was uncertain. I desperately tried not to think about it, but spinal injuries were the kiss of death for many athletes, and I knew it. I had enough money saved up from sponsorships and medal awards that we could live comfortably for a few years, but I would need to start thinking of a more stable job to support my family.

Family.

I groaned, running my fingers through my hair. This wasn't me. None of this was me. How had my life derailed so quickly? Gymnastics *was* my life, and now what could I do? Coaching? The thought of becoming Sam and dealing with someone like me made me want to panic. My eyes darted around the room. Wasn't it bigger just a few minutes ago? I felt trapped in a shoebox, contemplating marrying a woman I barely knew and raising a child with her. Now. When my professional life was *over. What the actual fuck?* I buried my face in my hand.

The door burst open and Corrine walked back in. "Are you all right, Mr. Phoenix?"

I shook my head, my face still covered. I couldn't breathe. My chest burned. I felt cool hands on mine, trying to uncover my face. "Breathe, sir. You're having a panic attack. Your heart rate is much too high right now. Do I need to call your doctor?"

I nodded. He needed to come tell me what the hell was wrong with me and if I had a shot at rehabilitation.

As if on cue, we both heard the sound of a throat clearing at the door. A man stood there, stony-faced, gripping a burgundy hardbound folder. *Dr. Clarke, MD* was emblazoned on his white lab coat.

"Mr. Phoenix, why are you alarming the monitor tech?" The emerging grin took the sting out of his harsh words.

"Didn't know I was." The room was still too small, still oppressive, but I was quickly calming. Corrine stepped out and returned a moment later to switch out IV bags.

"Do you have panic attacks often?"

"No," I answered. I almost never had them.

He nodded. "I was reviewing your X-rays. You really did a number on yourself. You have two compression fractures, one on your L5 vertebrae and a smaller one on your L4." He opened the binder and flipped a few pages. "And dislocated your shoulder, which obviously you knew."

I stared back at him, my mind blank, struggling to comprehend what he was saying. My last bit of strength evaporated as the weight of his words struck home. "I've broken my back?" I whispered.

"Compression fractures, technically. In layman's terms, yes. The good news is it's definitely not the worst thing you could do to yourself."

"How do you figure?"

"Well, for starters, you're not paralyzed. I'm not going to lie to you, this is going to hurt for quite some time, but it isn't a full break, and you have every chance for a full recovery and pain-free life. Most people with this injury are able to live perfectly normal lives. I'm going to prescribe you some pain medicines and muscle relaxers, and a back brace. You'll need to see an osteopath and perhaps an orthopedic surgeon, depending on how things go. They will determine whether you can get by with physical therapy in a few months or if you'll need surgery. For now, just take it easy and try to move as little as possible."

"You're discharging me?" Thank God. I wanted out of here.

"I think there's little we can do for you here, other than to continue giving you pain medication, which you can give yourself at home. As long as you're careful, you're good to go. Is there someone who can pick you up?"

"Sam, my coach. Doctor Clarke?"

"Yes?"

"What are the chances I will heal enough to be able to compete again?"

Doctor Clarke didn't answer for a long time. "Never say never, son. I don't want to raise your hopes with false promises. Let's just focus on reaching that 'pain free' status for the time being."

I nodded. I knew it was a long shot now, but hearing it out loud sucked. I shouldn't have asked.

The doctor left. The pain didn't seem anywhere near as unbearable as it had been. *Of course. Corrine must have started the pain meds.* I spotted a phone on a table to my left and pulled the whole thing onto the bed so I could dial Sam.

CHAPTER EIGHTEEN

"Lily? Are you here?" I called as I opened the door. My home felt strange after I'd left in such a rush two nights ago. She hadn't been answering her phone. I worried that she'd grown tired of waiting for me and left.

I had left the hospital in the early morning. After filling my prescriptions and picking up the back brace, I'd had Sam stop at a jewelry store. He'd adamantly tried to stop me, telling me I shouldn't make life decisions while under the influence of pain medicines, but I ignored him. I'd lost gymnastics. I'd be damned if I lost Lily, too.

I had the feeling Sam wanted to scold me for allowing myself to lose focus at *the* worst possible time, but he—correctly—decided I was punishing myself enough.

"I'm sorry I didn't get back to you sooner. I've been in the hospital." I held out the bouquet of roses and lilies I'd picked up for her. She stared at them as if she'd never seen flowers before.

"I saw. I was watching you compete." Her voice was flat, as though she were half asleep or drugged. My eyes narrowed.

"You saw? I've been trying to call you."

"I shut off my phone. I've been tired. Are you okay?"

"No, but we'll figure it out. These are for you." I wiggled the arrangement at her, but she still didn't take them. What was it with her and flowers? I was going to end up with a complex at this rate. "Please take them, Lily. This is not the most comfortable position to be standing in." I grimaced to demonstrate my point.

"Oh, I'm sorry." She took them and stared at them blankly.

"I'm sorry I left the other night. It was wrong of me."

"Where did you go?"

"John's."

"I'm sorry you felt the need to go, too. I'm sorry you didn't trust me enough to stay and work it out."

"Lily, it wasn't about trust. It just came as a huge shock. Can't you understand? You'd already had time to adjust. I didn't."

She nodded, tightening her grip around the bouquet.

"Look, I've been doing a lot of thinking since then, and I have a question for you."

Her eyes widened. I wasn't sure if she was happy, afraid, or some combination of the two. Only thing to do now was to press on.

"I'm sorry. I'd kneel, but it hurts and I'm not positive I'd be able to get back up again. We haven't known each other long, but our time together has been... nice. I want more of it. We can create a life together, and I want to be there for you and our child. You've said you love me. Well, I love you, too. I want to spend the rest of my life getting to know everything about you." I paused to clear my throat.

"Lily Campbell, will you do me the honor of being my wife?" I opened the ring box and held it out to her.

She dropped the flowers on the floor, causing some of them to spill out of the green cellophane wrapping. The chaotic way the fragile buds splayed on the floor reflected my frayed nerves. I forced myself to look at her face, noticing the blood had drained away, leaving her as pale as the white sand Florida beaches were famous for. Her mouth hung open. If the situation hadn't been so serious, her expression would have been comical–a perfect caricature of shock.

I waited for her to pull herself together. I knew my question had come as a surprise, but this was the right thing to do. I'd stay by her side and we'd raise our baby together.

Finally, her mouth closed, and color returned to her cheeks. She seemed to have gained back some of her composure. I waited patiently for her to accept and put me out of my misery.

"Oh, Xander... no."

To be continued...

ABOUT THE AUTHOR

David S. Scott is a new author of erotica and erotic romance novels. After fishing his debut novels, *Deep in You* and its sequel *Deeper in You*, he is moving on to several other projects, including an erotic paranormal tentatively titled *Obsidian Angel.* He is in his mid-thirties and happily married, and has a bit of a wicked sense of humor. When not writing, David can be found reading a variety of genres or playing "nerd games" like Dungeons and Dragons with his friends. David loves interacting with people and meeting new friends, so please be sure to follow him on his author page:

https://www.facebook.com/AuthorDavidScott